Dogs, Dogs, DOGS

Dogs, Dogs, DOGS

Stories of Challengers and Champions, Heroes and Hunters, Warriors and Workers

Stories selected by
PHYLLIS R. FENNER, comp.

Illustrated by
MANNING DE V. LEE

cop. 5

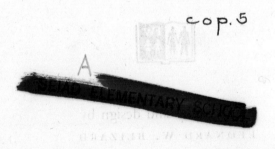

FRANKLIN WATTS, INCORPORATED
Publishers, 119 West 57th Street, New York 19, N. Y.

For
Chris and her dog

CONTENTS

ILLUSTRATIONS

ACKNOWLEDGMENTS

To Catherine Cate Coblentz and *Story Parade* for *The Dog Who Chose A Prince,* and to Mark Hager and *Story Parade* for *The Champions.* Copyright 1946, 1950 by Story Parade, Inc.

To Hilda Ollivant for *The Shepherd's Trophy* from *Bob, Son of Battle,* by Alfred Ollivant. Copyright 1889 by Hilda Ollivant.

To Holiday House for *Red's Education* from *Big Red,* by Jim Kjelgaard, copyright 1945 by Jim Kjelgaard; and for *Ne-Nu-Ka* from *Hudson Bay Express,* by Robert Davis, copyright 1942 by Robert Davis.

To The Macmillan Company for *For Love of a Man* from *The Call of the Wild,* by Jack London. Copyright 1903 by The Macmillan Company.

To Doubleday & Company, Inc. for *Gun Shy* from *Us and the Duchess,* by Edward Fenton, copyright 1945, 1946, 1947 by Edward Fenton; for *Pot Likker's First Fox Hunt* from *The Haunted Hound,* by Robb White, copyright 1950 by Robb White; and for *The Coming of Lad* from *The Heart of a Dog,* by A. P. Terhune, copyright 1924 by Doubleday & Company, Inc. Reprinted by permission of Doubleday & Company, Inc.

ACKNOWLEDGMENTS

To Appleton-Century-Crofts, Inc. for *Gulliver the Great* from *Gulliver the Great*, by Walter A. Dyer. Reprinted by permission of the publishers.

To The McGraw-Hill Book Company, Inc. for *Always Reddy*, from *Always Reddy*, by Marguerite Henry. Copyright 1947.

To Julian Messner, Inc. for *As Handsome Does* from *Handy of the Triple S*, by Genevieve Torrey Eames. Copyright April 27, 1949 by Genevieve Torrey Eames. Reprinted by permission of Julian Messner, Inc.

To Franklin Watts, Inc. for *Wild Hunter* from *Wild Hunter*, by K. C. Randall. Copyright 1951 by K. C. Randall.

To Harcourt, Brace and Company, Inc. for *Bat* from *Bat*, by Stephen W. Meader. Copyright 1939 by Harcourt, Brace and Company, Inc.

Man's Best Friend

What is the best kind of dog to own? That question could start a war. Well, the best kind of dog to own is the kind you have. Relax!

Oftentimes you hear that certain kinds of dogs are not friendly. Or other breeds are cross to children. But people who know dogs say that all dogs are equally good if they are treated properly and are well trained—that, just as with people, you will find individual dogs that have temperament.

If you live in the country, where dogs can run free, it is fun to have a big dog, a collie or boxer, a great Dane or even a Saint Bernard. If you like to hunt, a bird dog is the answer. If you live in an apartment, you'll probably choose a nice affectionate bulldog, or a Scottie, or even a "toy" dog. Just a "mutt" can bring great joy to his owner, for he can be just as intelligent, just as faithful, as a pedigreed dog. Whatever dog you have will bring you joy.

These stories are about many kinds of dogs: huskies pulling heavy sledges in the arctic; shepherd dogs winning trophies for their handling of sheep; fights between dogs and wild animals; stories of hunting dogs; of dogs' faithfulness to man.

It is said that many, many years ago, oh, sometime between the time when Moses was found in the bulrushes and when Columbus discovered America, Santa Claus had a Christmas party for the animals. When he asked the dog what he wanted for a present, the dog replied: "Give me faithfulness. Make me man's best friend."

Santa must have given him what he wanted, for surely the dog is the most faithful of all the animals, and often has proved that he is man's best friend.

P. F.

Dogs, Dogs, DOGS

The Champions

by MARK HAGER

It was a little while before dawn. Father and I stepped out in the yard and looked up at the cold March stars.

"Clear," Father remarked, "a good day to see the fight. I hope Acy Carter doesn't back out."

And then we heard the bugle note from Acy Carter's shotgun barrel. He blew the blast from the crest of the Wilson Ridge, which was the near cut from his house to ours.

"Glad he's getting here," Father said, "so we can start before daylight."

But before he said more, we heard another sound, and this time the sound was thin and high and quivering —the scream of a mountain lion. It came from high on the ridges in the thin moonlight.

"Old Scratch!" Father said, almost in a whisper. "He's answered Acy's blast from the shotgun."

And while Father spoke, there came another sound from the top of the Wilson Ridge. The sound was hoarse,

This story is from STORY PARADE magazine

3

deep, and full, and it echoed across the countryside. It was Blitz, challenging Old Scratch. I shivered in the moonlight and wondered if Blitz would be equal to the fight.

I knew that Blitz was no ordinary dog. Acy had gotten him to stand on the scales one day down at old Mr. Ponder's store, and Blitz had tipped the scales at exactly 59 pounds. In color he was the pale, milky blue of moonlight on green leaves, and on the moonlit ridges under the trees Blitz moved with the softness and agility of a shadow.

Yet when no battle brewed, Blitz was gentle. He was the pride and the glory of the neighborhood children. He'd go to school and lie in the big pile of leaves at the upper side of the steps, and let the children ride on his back.

All of which is one reason the neighbors had, for a whole year now, persuaded Acy Carter never to let Blitz fight Old Scratch.

The women and the children said Blitz was too gentle. But I knew better. I'd seen Blitz when danger threatened from the dark shadows of the woods. I knew how his eyes turned red, and his hair would rise like wheat stubble along his backbone, and his muscles would swell. And if he growled, his sharp, pointed teeth showed white like hot steel.

But still, I wasn't sure, for Old Scratch was no ordinary catamount. The womenfolks could tell you the most about

 4

him, for no hunter, armed with a gun, had ever gotten close enough even to get a good look at him.

But the women got to see him. It would be when the menfolks had taken the guns and gone to the hills to hunt, that Old Scratch would come down around the houses.

I recollect the day Father had been hunting. He came in about the time we children got home from school. As he laid his rifle back in the rack over the door, my mother said, "Hereafter, I wish you'd leave the gun at home."

Father looked startled. "Why?"

"I intend to learn to shoot it."

"What you aimin' to shoot?" he asked.

"Why, Old Scratch," she said. "He came again today. I heard the guinea hen scream, but I couldn't do a thing. When I looked out, Old Scratch had one of my geese by the neck. He didn't bother to kill it. It flopped and flopped, but he carried it off just the same. And, do you know, that beast had the brass to stop by the gate and look at me!"

Father said, "Did you get a good look at him?"

"His eyes are green," Mother said, "like two green, glassy marbles. He's got a white spot on his breast and, if I can learn to shoot that rifle, I intend to send a bullet through that white spot."

And Will Perdue would make you shiver when he'd tell of the time Old Scratch ventured to his house when

5

Mrs. Perdue and the children were alone there. This time he had a whole pack of young wild cats with him, and one half-way in size between the kittens and Old Scratch. Mrs. Perdue, in her excitement, grabbed the shotgun and fired, but she never could find any sign of where she hit, and she reckoned afterward, she may have just fired in the air. Anyhow, that aroused Will Perdue's coon dog, a big, vicious bluetick named Drive, and he came from the chimney corner. The blast of the gun, the dog, and the noisy guinea hens, put the pack of catamounts to flight, and they all got away except the middle-sized one, a female, which they guessed was the mother of the pack. Old Drive killed her, and made quite a name for himself.

But what made you shiver was that the very next night, Will Perdue heard Old Drive give one pitiful squall from his bed in the chimney corner and, by the time Will got his gun and lit the lantern, he found only a bloody streak of hair. Old Scratch had sneaked up, surprised Old Drive, nailed him with a death hold, and taken his vengeance.

This is why my mother came out when she heard Acy Carter's bugle note from his gun barrel, and she stood in the yard and waited until he came in on the frosty grass of our yard, holding Blitz. You could see Blitz's breath on the cold March air in the moonlight.

"Don't do it," my mother said to Acy Carter. "You know what Old Scratch did to Will Perdue's dog, and he was a pretty vicious dog at that."

6

"Blitz will kill him," Acy said. "Never you fear."

I admired Acy Carter's faith in Blitz, but I don't think Father shared it, for he remarked, "You don't have to do this, Acy. After all, you know there's never been a beast ever stood on four legs more vicious or dangerous."

Mother said, "He's got the advantage, Acy. A dog only has teeth. Old Scratch has got long blue claws. I saw 'em!"

Acy said, "And you all have never seen a dog such as Blitz. You never saw him crush coons' heads. I have. You all never saw him fling a six-foot rattler for thirty yards. You . . ."

Right there Acy was interrupted, for the catamount on the ridge was impatient for the fight. Again there came on the thin March air, from the pale moonlit domain of Old Scratch, the scream of defiance. It came sharp, like a needle stabbing.

Blitz went rigid, and I held the lantern and saw the stiff bristles rise on his back. I saw him plant his wide-set feet on the frozen ground.

He was broad-shouldered, and wide between the eyes, his ankles crooked, and his dew-claws low and sharp. His muscles swelled and quivered, and the great dog shivered. With all the vengeance a dog can put in his voice, he gave answer, and surged at the leash.

Acy started to unleash the dog.

"Don't yet," Father said. "It's just breaking day. I want to see the fight. We'll lead him up the ridge."

7

Acy said, "But the catamount will go back to the cliffs when day breaks."

"No, he won't," said Father. "Old Scratch knows as well as we do what's up. He's waiting." Father stepped into the door and reached for his rifle.

Acy said, "You don't need it. I won't let you shoot him. I only brought my shotgun to make him jump out of trees when Blitz makes him climb."

Father agreed, and we crossed our back field. "From the top of the next rise," Father said, "we should be within sight of him."

We climbed over a fence, ducked and twisted our way under and around the bamboos and the blackjacks. It opened up a little on the rise, and it was lighter.

Blitz squatted, shivered, and growled, and we looked.

Not a hundred yards above us, in the wide open and on the half-submerged trunk of a log across an old sheep trail, sat the catamount, waiting.

It was the first clear-cut view I'd ever had of him, and I could see the white spot on his breast, and the green eyes, of which my mother had spoken.

"Hadn't you better take a shot at him and save the dog?" Father said.

Acy Carter said, "The first crack belongs to Blitz."

Father said, "I reckon it's too far anyhow for a shotgun."

Acy Carter pulled the lug on the snap spring and unleashed the dog. He didn't break loose in a run, barking

8

The crouched beast never batted an eye but waited in utter
confidence

and yelping. Only an amateur would do that. Instead, he half crawled, digging in with his feet, ever ready for the spring. Now and then the old dog would look back with one eye over his shoulder, as if to receive a sign of assurance from Acy Carter.

Low, but firmly, Acy would say, "Take him, Blitz. Kill him, old boy!"

I shivered. My father shivered. As well as you could tell from the distance we were from the crouched beast, he never batted an eye, but waited in utter confidence.

From the distant barnyards came the crow of roosters, and now and then on the thin frosty air came the coo of a dove, thin and frail as the song of a beetle's wings.

Blitz crawled on. He came to the lower end of the log, but he knew he didn't have the claws for logs, and slowly, working his feet, he crawled up by the side of the log, keeping some six feet away from it. Then we could detect the slightest motion of the catamount, fixing its feet for the spring. Blitz never looked back now. He never seemed to take his eyes from the green eyes of Old Scratch.

Then came the spring. From what we could see, the catamount sprang first, but Blitz met him. The two beasts came together six feet from the earth. They did not lock. They seemed to hit and bounce from each other as if they were made of rubber, each seeming to land on his back.

Carefully, slowly, the two beasts regained their feet, turned to face each other, and gazed for a moment. I wondered about their feelings. I wondered why they hadn't locked, but you could tell they were sparring, measuring, feeling out and, with the same cool deliberation, they squared off.

Again they came together in the air. We moved quickly to get closer. Each time Old Scratch lunged, he only met Blitz's strong paws, and each time it seemed as if Blitz would pin the beast under his strong forepaws. But Old Scratch, being just as wily, knew his danger, and eluded it, once and again.

The third stroke we were close enough to see some pale hair fly from Blitz's neck, but Old Scratch had to make a desperate effort to get from under the great dog's paws. As he did, he let out the slightest scream of hurt, and I think the pointed teeth of Old Blitz scraped through his fur.

The fourth time they came down in a bamboo patch and locked for a good ten seconds.

"Blitz has pinned him," Acy Carter said. But no sooner had he spoken the words than the catamount got his hind feet loose and sent Blitz over on his back. Old Scratch had never before tackled a dog that wouldn't holler and wouldn't quit and, when Blitz got up and crouched for the fifth spring, the great cat's eyes turned glassy. He turned his head quickly to the right and to the left, and started up the hill by the side of the big log, but Blitz nailed him. This time they rolled over the brink of the crest toward a ravine, and they were tumbling, going

round and round and over and over, and you couldn't tell what was happening, except that you could see the hair flying on the frosty air. Yet no sound came from the fighting beasts.

We hurried to get to the brink of the ravine and, as we did, Old Scratch climbed a leaning oak.

"He's took a tree," said Acy. "Blitz will get him—he's whipped him."

Father said, "Look at your dog, Acy—he's bleeding all over."

But Acy didn't. He had his eyes on the catamount. "I'll make him jump," Acy said. "He can't do that."

Acy raised his gun but, before he could shoot, Old Scratch jumped from the leaning oak, landing on a log on the other side of the ravine. Almost at the same moment, Blitz crossed on a log at the upper end of the ravine, and he was on the great cat's tail, and gaining. It was a still and curious fight, as if it belonged to these two beasts alone.

They crossed the next ridge and were gone, as we ran around the upper end of the ravine and followed, falling every few steps on the dry frosty leaves.

When we topped the next ridge, they had both disappeared in the laurel thicket.

"Blitz must have caught him along here somewhere," said Acy, tracking the beasts by the blood on the frosty leaves.

 12

We stopped, stood still, but could hear no sound of Blitz or Scratch. We clambered on among the laurels.

By now, Acy was far out in front. After he was out of our sight in the laurels, he called back, "I found where Blitz caught him," he said, and we hurried to where he was.

But before we got to the place, we could hear Acy slashing the bushes and laurels far down below us. We came upon the sign. We saw where the beasts had rolled and tumbled and fought. We saw hairs on the briars and the bloodstains on the laurels and blackjacks.

It was rough, and almost impossible of passage, and Father panted for breath, and then he called, "Hey, Acy! Found 'em?" Acy Carter didn't answer.

My father called again, but there was no answer from man or beast.

We started down hill in the direction Acy had gone, following the animals. We found where he dropped his gun and then we heard him. He didn't speak, but we heard him as he came through the bushes.

Father was tall enough to see.

"Acy's got Blitz on his shoulder," Father said. He swallowed, then he hollered, "Hurt?"

"He's dead," said Acy, as he appeared, carrying Blitz. Cool and mild, he said it. He came up to us. "Hold him a minute," Acy said.

Father took the great limber dog in his arms, and Acy

13

Carter pulled off his coat, and laid it on a level place on the frosty leaves. He took Blitz and laid him on it, like a sleeping baby.

I looked at Acy Carter's face. He was crying, not making any noise.

"Pity," Father said, and studied a minute, and then went on, "as I said, I don't believe ever a dog stood on four feet that can kill that catamount."

Acy swiped his blue shirt sleeve across his face.

"Yes, they was," he said, his eyes cast down on the old dog. "Blitz killed him. He's down there, too. Dead. I reckon they both had grit, 'cause they stuck it out till they died."

Acy Carter began to look under the laurel bushes and I stood and shivered watching him. I thought he acted a little crazy, but then I noticed he had found a deep pile of rocks near a clump of laurel. Then he wrapped his coat carefully about the torn and bleeding body of his old dog. He pinned it with an old brass safety pin, and he buried the old dog deep in the rocks. When this was done, he arose and blew his nose, and we walked home together, without a word.

And of mornings even now, when the moonlight is thin and the shadows move on the ground, I stand in our yard and think of the great blue dog buried in his master's coat among the laurels.

14

The Shepherds' Trophy

by ALFRED OLLIVANT

CUP Day.

It broke calm and beautiful, no cloud on the horizon, no threat of storm in the air; a fitting day on which the Shepherds' Trophy must be won outright.

And well it was so. For never since the founding of the Dale Trials had such a concourse been gathered together on the north bank of the Silver Lea. From the Highlands they came; from the far Campbell country; from the Peak; from the county of many acres; from all along the silver fringes of the Solway; assembling in that quiet corner of the earth to see the famous Gray Dog of Kenmuir fight his last great battle for the Shepherds' Trophy.

By noon the gaunt Scaur looked down on such a gathering as it had never seen. The paddock at the back of the Dalesman's Daughter was packed with a clammering,

This story is from BOB, SON OF BATTLE, by Alfred Ollivant

15

chattering multitude: animated groups of farmers; bevies of solid rustics; sharp-faced townsmen; loud-voiced book-makers; giggling girls; amorous boys,—thrown together like toys in a sawdust bath; whilst here and there on the outskirts of the crowd, a lonely man and wise-faced dog, come from afar to wrest his proud title from the best sheep-dog in the North.

At the back of the enclosure was drawn up a formida-ble array of carts and carriages, varying as much in quality and character as did their owners. There was the squire's landau rubbing axle-boxes with Jem Burton's modest moke-cart; and there Viscount Birdsaye's flaring barouche side by side with the red-wheeled wagon of Kenmuir.

In the latter, Maggie, sad and sweet in her simple summer garb, leant over to talk to Lady Eleanour; while golden-haired wee Anne, delighted with the surging crowd around, trotted about the wagon, waving to her friends, and shouting from very joyousness.

Thick as flies clustered that motley assembly on the north bank of the Silver Lea. While on the other side the stream was a little group of judges, inspecting the course.

The line laid out ran thus: the sheep must first be found in the big enclosure to the right of the starting flag; then up the slope and away from the spectators; around a flag and obliquely down the hill again; through a gap in the wall; along the hillside, parallel to the Silver

16

Lea; abruptly to the left through a pair of flags—the trickiest turn of them all; then down the slope to the pen, which was set up close to the bridge over the stream.

The proceedings began with the Local Stakes, won by Rob Saunderson's veteran, Shep. There followed the Open Juveniles, carried off by Ned Hoppin's young dog. It was late in the afternoon when, at length, the great event of the meeting was reached.

In the enclosure behind the Dalesman's Daughter the clamour of the crowd increased tenfold, and the yells of the bookmakers were redoubled.

"Walk up, gen'lemen, walk up! the ole firm! Rasper? Yessir—twenty to one bar two! Twenty to one bar two! Bob? What price, Bob? Even money, sir—no, not a penny longer, couldn't do it! Red Wull? 'oo says Red Wull?"

On the far side the stream is clustered about the starting flag the finest array of sheep-dogs ever seen together.

"I've never seen such a field, and I've seen fifty," is Parson Leggy's verdict.

There, beside the tall form of his master, stands Owd Bob o' Kenmuir, the observed of all. His silvery brush fans the air, and he holds his dark head high as he scans his challengers, proudly conscious that to-day will make or mar his fame. Below him, the mean-looking, smooth-coated black dog is the unbeaten Pip, winner of the re-nowned Cambrian Stakes at Llangollen—as many think the best of all the good dogs that have come from the

17

sheep-dotted Wales. Beside him that handsome sable collie, with the tremendous coat and slash of white on throat and face, is the famous MacCallum More, fresh from his victory at the Highland meeting. The cobby, brown dog, seeming of many breeds, is from the land o' the Tykes—Merry, on whom the Yorkshiremen are laying as though they loved him. And Jess, the wiry black-and-tan, is the favourite of the men of the Derwent and Dove. Tupper's big blue Rasper is there; Londesley's Lassie; and many more—too many to mention: big and small, grand and mean, smooth and rough—and not a bad dog there.

And alone, his back to the others, stands a little bowed, conspicuous figure—Adam M'Adam; while the great dog beside him, a hideous incarnation of scowling defiance, is Red Wull, the Terror o' the Border.

The Tailless Tyke had already run up his fighting colours. For MacCallum More, going up to examine this forlorn great adversary, had conceived for him a violent antipathy, and straightway, had spun at him with all the fury of the Highland cateran, who attacks first and explains afterward. Red Wull, forthwith, had turned on him with savage, silent gluttony; bobtailed Rasper was racing up to join in the attack; and in another second the three would have been locked inseparably—but just in time M'Adam intervened.

One of the judges came hurrying up.

"Mr. M'Adam," he cried angrily, "if that brute of

18

yours gets fighting again, hang me if I don't disqualify him! Only last year at the Trials he killed the young Cossack dog."

A dull flash of passion swept across M'Adam's face. "Come here, Wullie!" he called. "Gin yon Hielant tyke attacks ye agin, ye're to be disqualified."

He was unheeded. The battle for the Cup had begun—little Pip leading the dance.

On the opposite slope the babel had subsided now. Hucksters left their wares, and bookmakers their stools, to watch the struggle. Every eye was intent on the moving figures of man and dog and three sheep over the stream.

One after one the competitors ran their course and penned their sheep—there was no single failure. And all received their just meed of applause, save only Adam M'Adam's Red Wull.

Last of all, when Owd Bob trotted out to uphold his title, there went up such a shout as made Maggie's wan cheeks to blush with pleasure, and wee Anne to scream right lustily.

His was an incomparable exhibition. Sheep should be humoured rather than hurried; coaxed rather than coerced. And that sheep-dog has attained the summit of his art who subdues his own personality and leads his sheep in pretending to be led. Well might the bosoms of the Dalesmen swell with pride as they watched their favourite phrase, "The brains of a mon and the way of a woman"; well might the crowd bawl their enthusiasm,

19

and Long Kirby puff his cheeks and rattle the money in his trouser pockets.

But of this part it is enough to say that Pip, Owd Bob, and Red Wull were selected to fight out the struggle afresh.

The course was altered and stiffened. On the far side the stream it remained as before; up the slope; round a flag; down the hill again; through the gap in the wall; along the hillside; down through the two flags; turn; and to the stream again. But the pen was removed from its former position, carried over the bridge, up the near slope, and the hurdles put together at the very foot of the spectators.

The sheep had to be driven over the plank-bridge, and the penning done beneath the very nose of the crowd. A stiff course, if ever there was one; and the time allowed, ten short minutes.

The spectators hustled and elbowed in their en-deavours to obtain a good position. And well they might; for about to begin was the finest exhibition of sheep-handling any man there was ever to behold.

Evan Jones and little Pip led off.

Those two, who had won on many a hard-fought field, worked together as they had never worked before. Smooth and swift, like a yacht in Southhampton Water;

20

round the flag, through the gap, they brought their sheep. Down between the two flags—accomplishing right well that awkward turn; and back to the bridge.

There they stopped: the sheep would not face that narrow way. Once, twice, and again, they broke; and each time the gallant little Pip, his tongue out and tail quivering, brought them back to the bridge-head.

At length one faced it; then another, and—it was too late. Time was up. The judges signalled; and the Welshman called off his dog and withdrew.

Out of sight of mortal eye, in a dip of the ground, Evan Jones sat down and took the small dark head between his knees—and you may be sure the dog's heart was heavy as the man's. "We did our pest, Pip," he cried brokenly, "but we're peat—the first time ever we've been!"

No time to dally.

James Moore and Owd Bob were off on their last run.

No applause this time; not a voice was raised; anxious faces; twitching fingers; the whole crowd tense as a stretched wire. A false turn, a wilful sheep, a cantankerous judge, and the gray dog would be beat. And not a man there but knew it.

Yet over the stream master and dog went about their business never so quiet, never so collected; for all the world as though they were rounding up a flock on the Muir Pike.

The old dog found his sheep in a twinkling and a wild,

21

scared trio they proved. Rounding the first flag, one bright-eyed wether made a dash for the open. He was quick; but the gray dog was quicker: a splendid *recover*, and a sound like a sob from the watchers on the hill.

Down the slope they came for the gap in the wall. A little below the opening, James Moore took his stand to stop and turn them; while a distance behind his sheep loitered Owd Bob, seeming to follow rather than drive, yet watchful of every movement and anticipating it. On he came, one eye on his master, the other on his sheep: never hurrying them, never flurrying them, yet bringing them rapidly along.

No word was spoken; barely a gesture made; yet they worked, master and dog, like one divided.

Through the gap, along the hill parallel to the spectators, playing into one another's hands like men at polo.

A wide sweep for the turn at the flags, and the sheep wheeled as though at the word of command, dropped through them, and travelled rapidly for the bridge.

"Steady!" whispered the crowd.

"Steady, man!" muttered Parson Leggy.

"Hold 'em, for God's sake!" croaked Kirby huskily. "D—n! I knew it! I saw it coming!"

The pace down the hill had grown quicker—too quick. Close on the bridge the three sheep made an effort to break. A dash—and two were checked; but the third went away like the wind, and after him Owd Bob, a gray streak against the green.

 22

Tammas was cursing silently; Kirby was white to the lips; and in the stillness you could plainly hear the Dalesmen's sobbing breath, as it fluttered in their throats.

"Gallop! they say he's old and slow!" muttered the Parson. "Dash! Look at that!" For the gray dog, racing like the nor' easter over the sea, had already retrieved the fugitive.

Man and dog were coaxing the three a step at a time toward the bridge.

One ventured—the others followed.

In the middle the leader stopped and tried to turn—and time was flying, flying, and the penning alone must take minutes. Many a man's hand was at his watch, but no one could take his eyes off the group below him to look.

"We're beat! I've won bet, Tammas!" groaned Sam'l. (The two had a long-standing wager on the matter.) "I allus knoo hoo 'twould be. I allus told yo' th' owd tyke —" then breaking into a bellow, his honest face crimson with enthusiasm: "Come on, Master! Good for yo', Owd Un! Yon's the style!"

For the gray dog had leapt on the back of the hindmost sheep; it had surged forward against the next, and they were over, and making up the slope amidst a thunder of applause.

At the pen it was a sight to see shepherd and dog working together. The Master, his face stern and a little whiter than its wont, casting forward with both hands, herding the sheep in; the gray dog, his eyes big and

23

bright, dropping to hand; crawling and creeping, closer and closer.

"They're in!—Nay—Ay—dang me! Stop 'er. Good Owd Un! Ah-h-h, they're in!" And the last sheep reluctantly passed through—on the stroke of time.

A roar went up from the crowd; Maggie's white face turned pink; and the Dalesmen mopped their wet brows. The mob surged forward, but the stewards held them back.

"Back, please! Don't encroach! M'Adam's to come!"

From the far bank the little man watched the scene. His coat and cap were off, and his hair gleamed white in the sun; his sleeves were rolled up; and his face was twitching but set as he stood—ready.

The hubbub over the stream at length subsided. One of the judges nodded to him.

"Noo, Wullie—noo or niver!—'Scots wha hae'!"—and they were off.

"Back, gentlemen! Back! He's off—he's coming! M'Adam's coming!"

They might well shout and push; for the great dog was on to his sheep before they knew it; and they went away with a rush, with him right on their backs. Up the slope they swept and round the first flag, already galloping. Down the hill for the gap, and M'Adam was flying ahead to turn them. But they passed him like a hurricane, and Red Wull was in front with a rush and turned them alone.

 24

"M'Adam wins! Five to four M'Adam! I lay agin Owd Bob!" rang out a clear voice in the silence.

Through the gap they rattled, ears back, feet twinkling like the wings of driven grouse.

"He's lost 'em! They'll break! They're away!" was the cry.

Sam'l was half up the wheel of the Kenmuir wagon; every man was on his toes; ladies were standing in their carriages; even Jim Mason's face flushed with momentary excitement.

The sheep were tearing along the hillside, all together, like a white scud. After them, galloping like a Waterloo winner, raced Red Wull. And last of all, leaping over the ground like a demoniac, making not for the two flags, but the plank-bridge, the white-haired figure of M'Adam.

"He's beat! The Killer's beat!" roared a strident voice.

"M'Adam wins! Five to four M'Adam! I lay agin Owd Bob!" rang out the clear reply.

Red Wull was now racing parallel to the fugitives and above them. All four were travelling at a terrific rate; while the two flags were barely twenty yards in front, below the line of flight and almost parallel to it. To effect the turn a change of direction must be made almost through a right angle.

"He's beat! he's beat! M'Adam's beat! Can't make it nohow!" was the roar.

From over the stream a yell—

"Turn 'em, Wullie!"

25

At the word the great dog swerved down on the flying three. They turned, still at the gallop, like a troop of cavalry, and dropped, clean and neat, between the flags; and down to the stream they rattled, passing M'Adam on the way as though he was standing.

"Weel done, Wullie!" came the scream from the far bank; and from the crowd went up an involuntary burst of applause.

"Ma word!"

"Did yo' see that?"

"By gob!"

It was a turn, indeed, of which the smartest team in the galloping horse-gunners might well have been proud. A shade later, and they must have overshot the mark; a shade sooner, and a miss.

"He's not been two minutes so far. We're beaten—don't you think so, Uncle Leggy?" asked Muriel Sylvester, looking up piteously into the parson's face.

"It's not what I think, my dear; it's what the judges think," the parson replied; and what he thought their verdict would be was plainly writ on his face for all to read.

Right on to the centre of the bridge the leading sheep galloped and—stopped abruptly.

Up above in the crowd there was utter silence; staring eyes; rigid fingers. The sweat was dripping off long Kirby's face; and, at the back, a green-coated bookmaker slipped his notebook in his pocket, and glanced behind him. James Moore, standing in front of them all, was the calmest there.

Red Wull was not to be denied. Like his forerunner he leapt on the back of the hindmost sheep. But the red dog was heavy where the gray was light. The sheep staggered, slipped, and fell.

Almost before it had touched the water, M'Adam, his face afire and eyes flaming, was in the stream. In a second he had hold of the struggling creature, and, with an almost superhuman effort, had half thrown, half shoved it on to the bank.

Again a tribute of admiration, led by James Moore.

The little man scrambled, panting, on to the bank and raced after sheep and dog. His face was white beneath the perspiration; his breath came in quavering gasps; his trousers were wet and clinging to his legs; he was trembling in every limb, and yet indomitable.

They were up to the pen, and the last wrestle began. The crowd, silent and motionless, craned forward to watch the uncanny, white-haired little man and the huge dog working so close below them. M'Adam's face was white; his eyes staring, unnaturally bright; his bent body projected forward; and he tapped with his stick on the ground like a blind man, coaxing the sheep in. And the Tailless Tyke, his tongue out and flanks heaving, crept and crawled and worked up to the opening, patient as he had never been before.

They were in at last.

27

There was a lukewarm, half-hearted cheer; then silence.

Exhausted and trembling, the little man leant against the pen, one hand on it; while Red Wull, his flanks still heaving, gently licked the other. Quite close stood James Moore and the gray dog; above was the black wall of people, utterly still; below, the judges comparing notes. In the silence you could almost hear the panting of the crowd.

Then one of the judges went up to James Moore and shook him by the hand.

The gray dog had won. Owd Bob o' Kenmuir had won the Shepherds' Trophy outright.

A second palpitating silence; a woman's hysterical laugh—and a deep-mouthed bellow rent the expectant air: shouts, screams, hat-tossings, back-clappings blending in a din that made the many-winding waters of the Silver Lea quiver and quiver again.

Owd Bob o' Kenmuir had won the Shepherds' Trophy outright.

Maggie's face flushed a scarlet hue. Wee Anne flung fat arms toward her triumphant Bob, and screamed with the best. Squire and parson, each red-cheeked, were boisterously shaking hands. Long Kirby, who had not prayed for thirty years, ejaculated with heartfelt earnestness, "Thank God!" Sam'l Todd bellowed in Tammas's ear, and almost slew him with his mighty buffets. Among the

Dalesmen some laughed like drunken men; some cried like children; all joined in that roaring song of victory.

To little M'Adam, standing with his back to the crowd, that storm of cheering came as the first announcement of defeat.

A wintry smile, like the sun over a March sea, crept across his face.

"We might a kent it, Wullie," he muttered, soft and low. The tension loosed, the battle lost, the little man almost broke down. There were red dabs of colour in his face; his eyes were big; his lips pitifully quivering; he was near to sobbing.

An old man—utterly alone—he had staked his all on a throw—and lost.

Lady Eleanour marked the forlorn little figure, standing solitary on the fringe of the uproarious mob. She noticed the expression on his face; and her tender heart went out to the lone man in his defeat.

She went up to him and laid a hand upon his arm.

"Mr. M'Adam," she said timidly, "won't you come and sit down in the tent? You look *so* tired! I can find you a corner where no one shall disturb you."

The little man wrenched roughly away. The unexpected kindness, coming at that moment, was almost too much for him. A few paces off he turned again.

"It's reel kind o' yer ladyship," he said huskily; and tottered away to be alone with Red Wull.

29

Meanwhile the victors stood like rocks in the tideway. About them surged a continually changing throng, shaking the man's hand, patting his dog.

Maggie had carried wee Anne to tender her congratulations; Long Kirby had come; Tammas, Saunderson, Hoppin, Tupper, Londesley—all but Jim Mason; and now elbowing through the press came squire and parson.

"Well done, James! well done, indeed! Knew you'd win! Told you so—eh, eh!" Then facetiously to Owd Bob: "Knew you would, Robert, old man! Ought to—Robert the Dev—mustn't be a naughty boy—eh, eh!"

"The first time ever the Dale Cup's been won outright!" said the parson; "and I dare say it never will again. And I think Kenmuir's the very fittest place for its final home, and a Gray Dog of Kenmuir for its winner."

"Oh, by the by!" burst in the squire. "I've fixed the Manor dinner for to-day fortnight, James. Tell Saunderson and Tupper, will you? Want all the tenants there." He disappeared into the crowd, but in a minute had fought his way back. "I'd forgotten something!" he shouted. "Tell your Maggie perhaps you'll have news for her after it—eh! eh!"—and he was gone again.

Last of all, James Moore was aware of a white, blotchy, grinning face at his elbow.

"I maun congratulate ye, Mr. Moore. Ye've beat us—you and the gentlemen—judges."

" 'Twas a close thing, M'Adam," the other answered.

"An' yo' made a gran' fight. In ma life I niver saw a finer turn than yours by the two flags yonder. I hope yo' bear no malice."

"Malice! Me? Is it likely? Na, na. 'Do onto ivery man as he does onto you—and somethin' over,' that's my motter. I owe ye mony a good turn, which I'll pay ye yet. Na na; there's nae good fechtin' agin fate—and the judges. Weel, I wush you well o' yer victory, Aiblins 'twill be oor turn next."

Then a rush, headed by Sam'l, roughly hustled the one away and bore the other off on its shoulders in boisterous triumph.

In giving the Cup away, Lady Eleanour made a prettier speech than ever. Yet all the while she was haunted by a white, miserable face; and all the while she was conscious of two black moving dots in the Murk Muir Pass opposite her—solitary, desolate, a contrast to the huzzaing crowd around.

That is how the champion challenge Dale Cup, the world-known Shepherds' Trophy, came to wander no more; won outright by the last of the Gray Dogs of Kenmuir—Owd Bob.

Red's Education

JIM KJELGAARD

Danny shifted his feet uncomfortably, and looked from the growing pile of dirt behind Red to Ross. The big setter, shoulder-deep in the hole, came to a turn and swerved to dig in this new direction. Danny reached down to twine his fingers in Red's collar, and drew him out of the hole.

"Come out of there," he said as roughly as he could.

The big dog stood panting as he gazed eagerly back down the hole. He made a little lunge as though to get back in, and Danny took a firmer grasp on his collar. Red bent his head, snuffling at the hot scent of the woodchuck in the hole. He whined eagerly. Ross's frozen face melted.

"Don't look so miserable about it," he said. "All the dog needs is some more teachin'. Any tenderfoot dog worth its salt is goin' to chase any kind of varmint. But, what a varmint dog this'n'll make!"

Danny gulped wretchedly. "What should I ought to do about it, Pappy?"

This story is from BIG RED, by Jim Kjelgaard

 32

"I'd give him a hidin'," Ross suggested seriously. "Now if'n he had a coon up a tree, I'd say let him go to it for all he's worth. But a varmint dog just can't stay at dens, and dig into every one he runs over. It takes too much time, and he's got to have a mind to stop it."

"But you can't give Red a lickin'!" Danny said desperately. "He's too smart and sensitive. Given I licked him he—he'd have no trust in me any more."

"Do tell!" Ross scoffed. "The dog was never born as didn't need to have sense licked into him at least once! But, as I said before, it's your dog. Bring him along and we'll get on with our fishin'."

Danny tugged on Red's collar, and the big setter strained backward toward the woodchuck hole. Danny dragged him from it, with Red protesting every step of the way, and when they had gone a hundred feet farther set him free. Red mounted an ant hill, and waved his plumed tail gently as he stared back toward the enticing den. Then he bounded to a moss-covered stump and smelled eagerly at it. Danny watched worriedly. A partridge dog had always to work within range of the hunter with him. And, of course, he must learn that partridges were the only game he could hunt. A dog that chased off after everything that crossed its path would be worse than useless.

But how to break him of this penchant for chasing varmints? Ross scoffed at the notion that a whipping would hurt him, but Danny knew better. Red had depths

33

of feeling and sensitivity that he had seen in no other dog, and he was proud. He wouldn't bear the lash any more than would a proud man. Danny looked worriedly at Ross's back. Sometimes it seemed that taking care of a highly bred dog brought more perplexing problems than anything else.

A small buck with ragged shreds of velvet clinging to his nearly matured antlers stepped from behind a beech tree and stood looking at them. Ross halted. The wind shifted, carried to the buck the scent of human beings, and with a rasping snort and a mighty leap he hoisted his white tail over his back and bounded away. Ross lifted the fishing rod he carried and with the imaginary gun followed the buck's course. He turned to grin.

"I could of had him," he said. "I could of had him three-four times while he tore through the trees that-away."

"Reckon you could, Pappy," Danny agreed. He had seen Ross bring down a buck running through slashings and a hundred yards away.

But he was studying Red, and heaved a great sigh of relief when the big setter betrayed no more than a passing interest in the buck. Deer scent, he knew, was the most pungent and exciting of any scent. Probably the hardest part of training any dog was to teach it not to run deer, and a dog that would run them was almost incurable. Danny had known of deer-running hounds to follow eagerly a scent two days old. But most hounds

34

took naturally to running deer, and most setters would do so only if their interest in deer was deliberately encouraged.

Two hundred yards farther on they flushed a doe and her adolescent fawn, and Red merely looked at them. He fell in beside Danny, and Danny reached gratefully down to stroke his ear.

They came to a sunlit meadow with a tangle of blackberry briers at one end and lush wild hay carpeting the remainder. Smokey Creek brushed the far side of the meadow and broadened into a long pool deep at the upper end and shallow at the lower. The shiners Ross wanted swarmed in the pool, and there were a few big bass there. Trout occasionally came into the pool, but preferred the more secluded and shadier portions of the creek.

Red left Danny's side and darted swiftly forward. He paused to look back, then advanced another ten feet. Ross stopped perplexedly, studying the dog as he lifted one forefoot and held his tail stiffly behind him. Danny exulted, and some of the anxiety that had sat so heavily upon him since he had discovered Red's bent for chasing varmints departed. He knew these signs. Red was on partridges now, and if he was somewhat clumsy about it he still was not doing badly for a dog that had had no training. Danny laid the rod and can of bait he carried on the ground, and stopped to pick up a stone. He walked quietly forward, grasped Red's collar, and cast the stone into

35

the small patch of blackberries at which he was pointing.

A partridge thundered up and soared across the meadow into the beech woods. Red whined, and twisted under Danny's restraining hand as he strove to follow. He reared with his front feet pawing the air. Danny held him.

"Easy," he murmured. "Don't get excited."

The big setter dropped back to earth and stood watching the place where the partridge had disappeared. As soon as Danny let him go, he raced out to cast around in circles and look for another bird. Danny watched him, leaping high in the tall grass so he could both see and scent, and turned to Ross with shining eyes.

"He had a partridge that time!" he ejaculated.

"I see he did." Ross looked disapprovingly at the ranging dog. "That's bad, Danny. A varmint dog shouldn't hunt nothin' but varmints. He sure oughtn't to go chasin' off after birds."

Danny said nothing.

Red came bounding back, and splashed shoulder-deep into the pool to lap thirstily at its crystal-clear water. He lay down to cool himself. A school of suckers moved sluggishly away from him, and a half dozen shiners darted erratically toward the bank, where they fell to nosing about the flat rocks that dotted the pool's bottom. Ross strung up his rod, baited the hook, and cast. Almost as soon as the line settled into the water a gentle tugging told of a bite. Ross struck, and his four-ounce rod curved slightly as he played a shiner in to the bank and slipped it into the live-bag that he had tied to a willow root beside the pool.

Red splashed out of the pool, stretched in the sun at Danny's feet, and went to sleep. Danny strung his own rod, cast, and almost immediately caught a fat chub. He put it in the live-bag, re-baited his hook, and caught another. There was no sport in catching chubs and shiners, but fish was the basis of almost every scent that he and Ross used on their far-flung trap-lines when winter came, and they took a major portion of their livelihood from trapping. For two hours they fished, until the live-bag was swarming with shiners.

Then, instead of the gentle tug that told of a shiner nibbling, Danny's line started straight across the pool. He let it go, feeling through the line and the wand-like rod that a big fish was on this time. The line stopped moving, and Danny waited tensely with two feet of slack looping from the reel.

"You better draw your line in," he warned Ross. "I got a bass out there fiddlin' with my bait, and he feels like a big'un. Given I ketch him, we won't eat side meat for supper."

Again the line began to move, and Danny struck hard. Out in the black pool, where the taut line dipped into the water, there was a swirling little ripple. Far out, a gleaming, bronze-black bass broke water and splashed back in as he strove to shake the hook. He bore toward

37

the bottom, and Danny paid out more line as he let him go. The rod, one that Ross himself had made, bent almost double. Danny elevated the tip, to let the fighting fish tire itself against the spring, and stripped in ten feet of line as the bass surged toward the bank. Red rose, and stood watching interestedly.

"Hang on!" Ross yelled. "He's a nice' un!"

"I'm a-tryin' to," Danny panted.

The bass turned back into the pool, and Danny paid out the line that he had retrieved. Again the fish broke water, rising high above the surface and falling back into it. He began to run in little circles that grew shorter as he became more tired, and Danny played him toward the bank. Slowly he fought the bass into the shallows, and Ross waded out to stand knee-deep in the water. He ran his fingers down Danny's taut line, fastened them in the bass's gills, and lifted him triumphantly free of the pool.

"Four pounds!" he gloated. "Danny, I disremember any such bass taken from Smokey Creek before."

"He sure is purty," Danny agreed. "And he'll go plenty good for supper, huh?"

"You bet," Ross agreed. "What say we catch a half dozen more shiners and go home? It's high on to evenin' time."

They fished ten minutes, added six more to the bag of shiners, and dismounted their rods. The sun was shining in the west, and a golden aureole glowed on the summits of the tallest mountains. Far back in the forests a fox

38

yelled, and the wan, sad cry of a mourning dove came from the nearby beeches. But aside from that the forest was strangely hushed. Red ranged ahead of them as they walked homeward, sniffling at likely cracks and crevices wherever he found them, and when they passed the woodchuck hole he sniffed long and deeply at it. But few of the wilderness creatures were moving.

They came to the fence, and Danny lifted it to let Red crawl under. Ross climbed over, and Danny was about to do so when a rabbit burst from a bunch of thistle and went bounding across the pasture.

With a wild yell, Red was after it. The rabbit lengthened out, his white tail twinkling as he called on every bit of speed he possessed. Red flew, tail close to the ground and head up as he strove to overtake this enticing quarry. Chained to their kennels, the four hounds bayed loud encouragement. Even Asa, the mule, overcame his customary indifference to everything sufficiently to raise his head and watch.

Danny yelled, "Red, come back here! Come back!"

The big setter paid no heed, but bounded on after the fleeing rabbit. A half jump ahead of the dog, it flashed beneath a rock pile and disappeared. With his hindquarters in the air and his front ones close to the ground, Red pawed futilely at the rocks. Danny ran up, grasped his collar, and jerked him roughly aside.

"You, Red! I dunno what I will do with you, anyhow!"

Ross walked up. "Goll ding it, I said I wouldn't med-

39

dle in the way you teach your dog. But he sure needs a hidin'. You let him sniff into dens and holes thataway, and he ain't never goin' to be no good for anything."

"Pappy, I won't whip that dog!"

Ross shrugged.

Red looked happily up, tongue lolling, tail wagging, and a bright, devilish gleam in his eye. Danny's heart melted. Red was smart, with all the heart and courage that anyone could ask for or expect to find in a dog. There must be some method, other than whipping, to wean him away from this sort of chasing and make him hunt partridges only. Danny gritted his teeth. It was up to him to find that method. He pulled Red into the house.

Ross took their catch of shiners into the shed, and began to prepare the trap-line scents that only he could make properly. Red went out to lie down on the porch. Danny skinned the bass, split it, and removed the heavy spinal bone. He laid the two halves in a pan of cold water and added a little salt. Red pushed the door open with his nose and came back in. Danny looked fondly at him.

"Rabbit-chaser," he murmured. "Darn old rabbit-chaser. When you goin' to get some sense into you?"

Red thumped the floor with his tail while Danny took the two halves of bass and laid them in a hot skillet. He sliced potatoes in another skillet, and put them on the stove to fry while he set the table. His hands covered with fish scales, Ross entered and washed. He took his home-made violin from its case, drew the bow across it a couple of times, and sat on a chair to coax from it the haunting strains of "Johnny O'Dare." Danny sang softly with him,

> "Johnny O'Dare the moon is glowin',
> The silver clouds in the sky are showin'
> And I sit alone but alone am knowin',
> You'll come home to me Johnny O'Dare."

He grinned. The day was gone, and with it all the doubts and perplexities it had brought. He, Ross, and Red, were alone with plenty to eat and a song in their hearts. It was enough. Danny put the cooked food on the table, and Ross returned the violin to its case. Both sat down to eat.

"What we goin' to do tomorrow, Pappy?" Danny asked.

"Mr. Haggin asked me to fetch him twenty-four quarts of blackberries," Ross said. "I better get at that come mornin'; he'll pay fifteen cents a quart. After that I won't be able to take any side jobs on account there's trap-lines that ain't staked out and I feel a ache for a varmint hunt. How would you like to chop down and trim a few trees for wood?"

"Sure. Fine."

Ross took a great forkful of the bass. "This is mighty tasty fish, Danny. By the way, do you consider that we should ought to let that Red dog run along when I take

41

the hounds on a varmint hunt? Ol' Mike could teach him some tricks, and he's smart enough to pick up where Mike leaves off."

Danny choked on the food in his mouth. "I, I just don't favor the notion of Red's runnin' with hounds."

Ross looked at him, a little resentfully. "Well, it's your dog."

Danny went out to sit on the porch, while Red sat beside him and poked his nose into Danny's cupped hand. This was mighty serious. Ross had his heart set on making Red a varmint dog, and Red just couldn't be a varmint dog. It was in him to hunt birds, nothing else. Danny's right arm stole out to encircle the big setter's neck.

"You got to be a bird dog," he said. "You chase them little varmints because it's fun, but at heart you're a bird hunter. I sure wish Pappy'd understand. How we goin' to make him?"

Ross was already in bed when Danny re-entered the cottage and sought his own cot. And, though Danny was up with the sun, Ross had risen, prepared his own breakfast, taken his picking pails, and departed for the blackberry thickets. Danny milked the cow, fed Asa and Red, ate a great heap of pancakes, and took a razor-keen double-bitted axe from its rack in the closet. He went outside, strung Asa's leather and chain into the singletree that dragged behind. Asa followed indifferently when Danny started toward a stand of yellow birch that had grown up in the beeches. Mr. Haggin, who owned most of the beech

Shouting at Red did no good

43

woods as well as the great Wintapi estate, didn't want any other trees cut as long as there was scrap wood like yellow birch around.

Red ranged before them, sniffling at likely thickets and bits of brush along the way. He came to a stiff point beside a clump of laurel, and held it while Danny flushed two partridges. Red made an eager little jump forward, and stopped. Danny forgot to breathe. The dog was smart, plenty smart, and getting the idea that it was not right to chase the partridges he pointed. Danny frowned. If only he would get the same idea about varmints! But how to teach him without resorting to violent methods?

"I think you're doin' it out of devilishness alone," Danny murmured, more to himself than to the dog. "Doggonit, Red, why can't you stop?"

A hundred feet farther on Red had an ecstatic time chasing a chipmunk that was rooting in the fallen leaves for beech-nuts, and a little beyond he tore through the woods after a fleeing rabbit. Danny swung his axe and lopped down the thick weeds that had grown up beside the trail. Shouting at Red, as he had proven yesterday, did no good. Maybe, after all, he would have to use the choke collar and drag rope. He came to the stand of yellow birch, hitched Asa to one, and set to work felling the slender little trees.

Most of the day he worked, chopping the birches down, trimming the branches from them, and piling them in a

44

great heap. In the middle of the afternoon he untied Asa, led him to the felled trees, hooked the chain around a dozen of them, and tightened it. He led the mule back down the trail, left the trees in the chip-littered wood yard behind the shanty, and went back for another load. Dusk had fallen when he went down the trail with the last of the trees, and blue smoke was rising lazily from the cabin's chimney. He led Asa to the wood yard, and was piling the trees on those already there, when Ross came from the cabin to stand silently watching.

"You got a right smart lot of wood," he finally observed. "You better give Asa a feed of grain and rub him down, too. I'll have some vittles for you when you come in."

Danny cared for the mule, hung the harness in the barn, and with Red padding beside him entered the house. Ross bent over the stove, and when Danny came in he turned to smile wanly.

"I bet you got a yen for grub," he said.

"I could eat," Danny admitted. "But I'm not so tired. Tell me about yourself. Did you see Mr. Haggin?"

"Yup." With studied deliberation Ross turned away from him and faced the stove. "I took him his berries. By the way, Danny, he wants you should bring that Red dog and come down in the mornin'. There's some sort of quality woman stayin' there, and I guess he wants she should see him."

"Why, sure. It's Mr. Haggin's dog. He's got the right to see him if he wants."

45

"Danny . . ."

"What?"

"I . . . Set down and eat your supper," Ross finished lamely. "You won't have nothin' else to do tomorrow. I'll take care of the wood you and Asa brought in."

"Two of us with a cross-cut'll get it sawed quicker," Danny said. "What's the matter with you, Pappy?"

"Nothin'. Set and eat."

Danny ate, and after eating strolled through the evening woods with Red while Ross washed the dishes. He was a little worried about his father. That Ross should even offer to wash the dishes was astounding in itself. Still, there didn't seem to be any physical difficulty; evidently Ross had something on his mind. When darkness fell, Danny went in to bed.

He was up very early, and scrubbed his face to the point of immaculateness in the tin basin. He put on a clean shirt and a fresh pair of trousers, and after breakfast, with Red frisking beside him, started down the Smokey Creek trail. A red fox leaped across the trail ahead of them, and Red dashed wildly to lunge at it. After ten minutes Red came back, panting heavily. Danny frowned and walked on. They broke out of the woods into the rolling acres of Mr. Haggin's estate, and started across them.

Red fell back to pace sedately at Danny's side, and Danny reached down to reassure himself by touching the dog's head. Of course Mr. Haggin was a mighty fine man,

 46

but just the same it was hard not to feel at least a little awed when approaching such magnificence as was to be encountered on his Wintapi estate. Danny saw two riders galloping on a pair of Mr. Haggin's blooded horses along a bridle trail, and looked carefully at them. One was Mr. Haggin himself, and the other looked like a woman. Danny stopped in front of the barn. The two riders galloped in, and Red backed uncertainly against his knees. A groom came forward to take their horses, and Mr. Haggin and his companion swung from their saddles to come toward Danny. Mr. Haggin's booming voice bridged the distance between them.

"Good morning, Danny."

"Mornin', sir. I brought Red down."

Danny was studying the woman. She was tall, slender, and moved with the easy grace of a sable. She was dressed in riding breeches, polished boots, and a silken shirt. Her black hair had blown back on her head, and her cheeks were flushed. Certainly it was the quality woman of whom Ross had spoken. Yet Danny twitched uncomfortably. There was something very hard and very cold about her, as though she had always had her own way and always intended to have it.

"Miss Grennan, meet Danny Pickett," Mr. Haggin said.

"Hello, Danny," the quality woman smiled.

"Howdy, ma'am," Danny mumbled.

"Miss Grennan's the manager of my Philadelphia

47

branch," Mr. Haggin explained. "There's the dog I was telling you about, Katherine, Champion Sylvester's Boy."

"Oh, Dick, what a gorgeous creature!"

The quality woman knelt beside Red, and put her hand on his ruff. Red backed a little nearer to Danny, to get away from the smell of the perfume she wore. Danny looked at her with miserable eyes, knowing now why Ross had been so perturbed last night. The quality woman rose to her feet.

"Dick, give him to me."

"Whoa there! Wait a minute. What would you do with a dog like that?"

"Dick, let me have him."

Mr. Haggin coughed, and looked away. He squirmed and coughed again. "Now, Katherine, your sense of acquisitiveness . . ."

"Oh, you silly! Let me have him for six months, and show him off in Philly."

"I can't let you have that dog."

"Why not?"

"Danny."

Katherine Grennan smiled again. "What do you say, Danny?"

"Well, I sure wouldn't like to see Red leave here."

The quality woman was very cold now, and very hard. "I know you wouldn't, Danny. But it isn't your dog, is it? It belongs to Mr. Haggin, doesn't it?"

 48

Danny said manfully, "Yes ma'am."

"There!" she said triumphantly. "Now let me have him, Dick."

Mr. Haggin looked at Danny. "Do you think she should take him?"

"It's your dog," Danny said.

"There, old iron man!" the quality woman said. "You can't have another thing to say. Anyhow, he'll be back in six months."

Mr. Haggin shrugged helplessly. "All right, Danny. Do you want to leave him now or bring him down in the morning?"

"Well," Danny hedged, "I could just as leave bring him in the mornin', and save you the bother of feedin' him tonight."

"Do that, Danny," the quality woman smiled. "I'll be leaving at eight o'clock."

With Red beside him, Danny turned miserably away. He swung from the trail to the foot of Misty Mountain, and started up its slope. When Red dashed after a squirrel, Danny only looked dully at him. The big dog might as well have his fun. Tomorrow morning he was going to Philadelphia, and that was almost as big as New York. There'd be no forest there, nothing except pavement and little patches of green grass that were called parks. With the back of his hand Danny wiped the tears from his eyes. The quality woman didn't really want a dog, or know what a fine dog was. She wanted Red because he

49

looked nice, and would complement her own faultlessly groomed self. Every morning, probably, she would take him walking on a leash and the rest of the time he'd spend chained to some little kennel where there was just enough grass for him to scratch in.

It wasn't right to take a dog like Red away from the life he was meant for.

The bushes moved, and Red dashed happily in to chase whatever small creature was moving them. A little farther on he pointed two grouse, and Danny didn't even try to keep him from running after them when they flushed. All day he walked, up Misty Mountain, down its other side, and into the nameless gullies and ravines that lay beyond. It was his last day with Red. True, the quality woman had said that she would bring him back in six months, but Danny didn't believe it. Once she got him, she'd find some excuse for keeping him. Darkness had fallen when Danny swung back to the clearing in the beech woods and stamped wearily into the cabin. Ross was there, sitting at the table and staring at the flickering kerosene lamp. He turned blankly around.

"The quality woman down to Mr. Haggin's," Danny explained dully. "Mr. Haggin give Red to her. She's takin' him come eight o'clock in the mornin'. I got to fetch him down then."

Ross nodded. "I figured she'd try to get her hooks in him given she saw him. I pegged her for that kind. What you goin' to do about it, Danny?"

50

"Take him down," Danny said hopelessly. "It's Mr. Haggin's rightful dog."

He sat miserably on a chair, pecked at the food that Ross put before him, and pillowed his chin in his hands. Ross filled and smoked his pipe, something he did only in times of great stress, and there was a long silence.

"You know what, Danny?" he said finally. "If I had the money cost of that dog, I'd buy him and give him to you."

"We haven't got seven thousand dollars," Danny said bitterly. "We haven't even got seventy dollars."

"That's right," Ross said tiredly.

Danny rose and sought his cot, praying for the sleep that would not come. Sleep brought forgetfulness, and if he could forget only for a few minutes . . . But the long night hours dragged dismally and endlessly on. Just before dawn he fell into a restless and dream-troubled slumber from which Ross awakened him.

"Danny, I don't want to bother you. But if you have to be down to Mr. Haggin's at eight o'clock, it's nearly quarter past seven."

"Sure, sure. Thanks for wakin' me, Pappy."

Danny got out of bed and Red padded eagerly in to greet him with lolling tongue and wagging tail. Danny tore his eyes away from the big setter, and put on the clean clothes he had worn yesterday. There must be no fumbling or faltering now—unless the quality woman wanted to walk into the country back of Stoney Lone-

51

some to claim her dog! Danny stooped to pat Red's fore-head, and with an effort walked past him to linger in front of the door.

"I—I'll have some vittles when I get back, Pappy," he said. "Likely it won't take me long."

"Sure."

Ross turned around to stare out of the window. Danny opened the door, and Red raced happily out. He dashed at a rabbit that was nibbling clover at the edge of the pasture, and ran it under the stone pile. After scratching at the unyielding stones a few seconds he ran down the trail to catch up with Danny. Danny walked stolidly forward, turning his head away from the dog. A powerful magnet seemed to be pulling him toward Stoney Lonesome, where he could take Red and where Mr. Haggin and the quality woman couldn't find him if he didn't want to be found. But that wouldn't be right. Red was Mr. Haggin's dog, and Mr. Haggin had a perfect right to do with him what he would.

Some tall grass beside the trail moved, and Red raced joyously down to investigate. He jumped into the grass, remained a moment, and came stumbling out. For a bit he stood in the trail, and rubbed his face in its gravelled bottom.

Danny said sternly, "Heel."

He marched steadily on, not looking around. Red had had his last run after a varmint. When he got to Philadelphia there might be a cat or two for him to chase. But certainly there would be nothing more. Danny took a deep breath, and plunged out of the forest onto Mr. Haggin's estate. He saw Mr. Haggin, standing with one foot on the running-board of a smart roadster, and the quality woman in it with her hands on the wheel. She looked curiously around, as Mr. Haggin said,

"Good morning, Danny."

"Mornin', sir."

The quality woman took a silk handkerchief from her purse and held it delicately against her nose. Red backed against Danny's knees, and Danny steeled his aching heart. The big setter did not want to go. But he must go. Danny stooped, put one arm around Red's chest and the other about his rear legs. He lifted him bodily, and deposited him on the polished leather seat beside the quality woman.

"Here's your dog, Ma'am," he murmured.

Suddenly and violently the quality woman recoiled. She grimaced, grabbed the silk handkerchief with both hands, and plastered it against her nose.

"Get that thing out of here!" she gasped.

Red hopped over the side of the car, and squeezed very close to Danny's legs. The woman turned furious eyes on Mr. Haggin, whose face had turned purple and whose mouth was emitting subdued gurgles.

"Dick, if this is your idea of a joke . . . !"

"Now, Katherine, I swear that I had nothing whatever to do with it."

53

The quality woman put her car in gear, stepped on the gas, and gravel spurted from beneath the wheels as she roared toward the road. Mr. Haggin gasped, and burst into gales of uncontrolled laughter. Danny watched wonderingly.

"Oh Lord!" Mr. Haggin said at last. "That's the best I ever saw! Katherine thought she knew everything, and found out that she still has something to learn. Take your dog and go back up into the beech woods, Danny. He's safe now."

But Danny had already gone, was racing up the Smokey Creek trail on winged feet, with Red gambolling happily beside him. A small rabbit hopped across the trail, and Red made a wide circle around it. Danny burst into the cabin.

"Pappy!" he yelled. "Pappy, I got Red back and I'm goin' to keep him. He don't chase varmints no more, either; he wouldn't run at a little old rabbit in the trail. That quality woman, she's gone and she don't want him, just because on the way down he jumped on a skunk! Can you imagine anybody not wantin' a dog like him just because he smells?"

Ross's eyes were shining, but he shook his head gravely. "City women are funny thataway," he observed. "I'm so glad for you, Danny. But you better take your dog down to the crick and wash him off. He do smell a bit, but in a couple of weeks you won't hardly notice it a'tall."

For Love of a Man

by JACK LONDON

It was beautiful spring weather, but neither dogs nor humans were aware of it. Each day the sun rose earlier and set later. It was dawn by three in the morning, and twilight lingered till nine at night. The whole day long was a blaze of sunshine. The ghostly winter silence had given way to the great spring murmur of awakening life. This murmur arose from all the land, fraught with the joy of living. It came from the things that lived and moved again, things which had been as dead and which had not moved during the long months of frost. The sap was rising in the pines. The willows and aspens were bursting out in young buds. Shrubs and vines were putting on fresh garbs of green. Crickets sang in the nights, and in the days all manner of creeping, crawling things rustled forth into the sun. Partridges and woodpeckers were booming and knocking in the forest. Squirrels were chattering, birds singing, and overhead honked the wild-fowl driving up from the south in cunning wedges that split the air.

This story is from THE CALL OF THE WILD, by Jack London

55

From every hill slope came the trickle of running water, the music of unseen fountains. All things were thawing, bending, snapping. The Yukon was straining to break loose the ice that bound it down. It ate away from beneath; the sun ate from above. Air-holes formed, fissures sprang and spread apart, while thin sections of ice fell through bodily into the river. And amid all this bursting, rendering, throbbing of awakening life, under the blazing sun and through the soft-sighing breezes, like wayfarers to death, staggered the two men, the woman, and the huskies.

With the dogs falling, Mercedes weeping and riding, Hal swearing innocuously, and Charles's eyes wistfully watering, they staggered into John Thornton's camp at the mouth of White River. When they halted, the dogs dropped down as though they had all been struck dead. Mercedes dried her eyes and looked at John Thornton. Charles sat down on a log to rest. He sat down very slowly and painstakingly what of his great stiffness. Hal did the talking. John Thornton was whittling the last touches on an axehandle he had made from a stick of birch. He whittled and listened, gave monosyllable replies, and, when it was asked, terse advice. He knew the breed, and he gave his advice in the certainty that it would not be followed.

"They told us up above that the bottom was dropping out of the trail and that the best thing for us to do was lay over," Hal said, in response to Thornton's warning to take no more chances on the rotten ice. "They told us we·

couldn't make White River, and here we are." This last with a sneering ring of triumph in it.

"And they told you true," John Thornton answered. "The bottom's likely to drop out at any moment. Only fools, with the blind luck of fools, could have made it. I tell you straight, I wouldn't risk my carcass on that ice for all the gold in Alaska."

"That's because you're not a fool, I suppose," said Hal. "All the same, we'll go on to Dawson." He uncoiled his whip. "Get up there, Buck! Hi! Get up there! Mush on!"

Thornton went on whittling. It was idle, he knew, to get between a fool and his folly; while two or three fools more or less would not alter the scheme of things.

But the team did not get up at the command. It had been long since passed into the stage where blows were required to rouse it. The whip flashed out, here and there, on its merciless errands. John Thornton compressed his lips. Sol-leks was the first to crawl to his feet. Teek followed. Joe came next, yelping with pain. Pike made painful efforts. Twice he fell over, when half up, and on the third attempt managed to rise. Buck made no effort. He lay quietly where he had fallen. The lash bit into him again and again, but he neither whined nor struggled. Several times Thornton started, as though to speak, but changed his mind. A moisture came into his eyes, and, as the whipping continued, he arose and walked irresolutely up and down.

57

This was the first time Buck had failed, in itself a sufficient reason to drive Hal into a rage. He exchanged the whip for the customary club. Buck refused to move under the rain of heavier blows which now fell upon him. Like his mates, he was barely able to get up, but, unlike them, he had made up his mind not to get up. He had a vague feeling of impending doom. This had been strong upon him when he pulled in to the bank, and it had not departed from him. What of the thin and rotten ice he had felt under his feet all day, it seemed that he sensed disaster close at hand, out there ahead on the ice where his master was trying to drive him. He refused to stir. So greatly had he suffered, and so far gone was he, that the blows did not hurt much. And as they continued to fall upon him, the spark of life within flickered and went down. It was nearly out. He felt strangely numb. As though from a great distance, he was aware that he was being beaten. The last sensations of pain left him. He no longer felt anything, though very faintly he could hear the impact of the club upon his body. But it was no longer his body, it seemed so far away.

And then, suddenly, without warning, uttering a cry that was inarticulate and more like the cry of an animal, John Thornton sprang upon the man who wielded the club. Hal was hurled backward, as though struck by a falling tree. Mercedes screamed. Charles looked on wistfully, wiped his watery eyes, but did not get up because of his stiffness.

John Thornton stood over Buck, struggling to control himself, too convulsed with rage to speak.

"If you strike that dog again, I'll kill you," he at last managed to say in a choking voice.

"It's my dog," Hal replied, wiping the blood from his mouth as he came back. "Get out of my way, or I'll fix you. I'm going to Dawson."

Thornton stood between him and Buck, and evinced no intention of getting out of the way. Hal drew his long hunting-knife. Mercedes screamed, cried, laughed, and manifested the chaotic abandonment of hysteria. Thornton rapped Hal's knuckles with the axe-handle, knocking the knife to the ground. He rapped his knuckles again as he tried to pick it up. Then he stooped, picked it up himself, and with two strokes cut Buck's traces.

Hal had no fight left in him. Besides, his hands were full with his sister, or his arms, rather; while Buck was too near dead to be of further use in hauling the sled. A few minutes later they pulled out from the bank and down the river. Buck heard them go and raised his head to see. Pike was leading, Sol-leks was at the wheel, and between were Joe and Teek. They were limping and staggering. Mercedes was riding the loaded sled. Hal guided at the gee-pole, and Charles stumbled along in the rear.

As Buck watched them, Thornton knelt beside him and with rough, kindly hands searched for broken bones. By the time his search had disclosed nothing more than

59

many bruises and a state of terrible starvation, the sled was a quarter of a mile away. Dog and man watched it crawling along over the ice. Suddenly, they saw its back end drop down, as into a rut, and the gee-pole, with Hal clinging to it, jerk into the air. Mercedes's scream came to their ears. They saw Charles turn and make one step to run back, and then a whole section of ice give way and dogs and humans disappear. A yawning hole was all that was to be seen. The bottom had dropped out of the trail.

John Thornton and Buck looked at each other.

"You poor devil," said John Thornton, and Buck licked his hand.

When John Thornton froze his feet in the previous December, his partners had made him comfortable and left him to get well, going on themselves up the river to get out a raft of saw-logs for Dawson. He was still limping slightly at the time he rescued Buck, but with the continued warm weather even the slight limp left him. And here, lying by the river bank through the long spring days, watching the running water, listening lazily to the songs of birds and the hum of nature, Buck slowly won back his strength.

A rest comes very good after one has travelled three thousand miles, and it must be confessed that Buck waxed lazy as his wounds healed, his muscles swelled out, and the flesh came back to cover his bones. For that matter, they were all loafing,—Buck, John Thornton, and Skeet and Nig,—waiting for the raft to come that was to carry them down to Dawson. Skeet was a little Irish setter who early made friends with Buck, who, in a dying condition, was unable to resent her first advances. She had the doctor trait which some dogs possess, and as a mother cat washes her kittens, so she washed and cleansed Buck's wounds. Regularly, each morning after he had finished his breakfast, she performed her self-appointed task, till he came to look for her ministrations as much as he did for Thornton's. Nig, equally friendly, though less demonstrative, was a huge black dog, half bloodhound and half deerhound, with eyes that laughed and a boundless good nature.

To Buck's surprise these dogs manifested no jealousy toward him. They seemed to share the kindliness and largeness of John Thornton. As Buck grew stronger they enticed him into all sorts of ridiculous games, in which Thornton himself could not forbear to join, and in this fashion Buck romped through his convalescence and into a new existence. Love, genuine passionate love, was his for the first time. This he had never experienced at Judge Miller's down in the sun-kissed Santa Clara Valley. With the Judge's sons, hunting and tramping, it had been a working partnership; with the Judge's grandsons, a sort of pompous guardianship; and with the Judge himself, a stately and dignified friendship. But love that was feverish and burning, that was adoration, that was madness, it had taken John Thornton to arouse.

This man had saved his life, which was something; but,

further, he was the ideal master. Other men saw to the welfare of their dogs from a sense of duty and business expediency; he saw to the welfare of his as if they were his own children, because he could not help it. And he saw further. He never forgot a kindly greeting or a cheering word, and to sit down for a long talk with them ("gas" he called it) was as much his delight as theirs. He had a way of taking Buck's head roughly between his hands, and resting his own head upon Buck's, of shaking him back and forth, the while calling him ill names that to Buck were loving names. Buck knew no greater joy than that rough embrace and the sound of murmured oaths, and at each jerk back and forth it seemed that his heart would be shaken out of his body so great was its ecstasy. And when, released, he sprang to his feet, his mouth laughing, his eyes eloquent, his throat vibrant with unuttered sound, and in that fashion remained without movement, John Thornton would reverently exclaim, "God! you can all but speak!"

Buck had a trick of love expression that was akin to hurt. He would often seize Thornton's hand in his mouth and close so fiercely that the flesh bore the impress of his teeth for some time afterward. And as Buck understood the oaths to be love words, so the man understood this feigned bite for a caress.

For the most part, however, Buck's love was expressed in adoration. While he went wild with happiness when Thornton touched him or spoke to him, he did not seek these tokens. Unlike Skeet, who was wont to shove her nose under Thornton's hand and nudge and nudge till petted, or Nig, who would stalk up and rest his great head on Thornton's knee, Buck was content to adore at a distance. He would lie by the hour, eager, alert, at Thornton's feet, looking up into his face, dwelling upon it, studying it, following with keenest interest each fleeting expression, every movement or change of feature. Or, as chance might have it, he would lie farther away, to the side or rear, watching the outlines of the man and the occasional movements of his body. And often, such was the communion in which they lived, the strength of Buck's gaze would draw John Thornton's head around, and he would return the gaze, without speech, his heart shining out of his eyes as Buck's heart shone out.

For a long time after his rescue, Buck did not like Thornton to get out of his sight. From the moment he left the tent to when he entered it again, Buck would follow at his heels. His transient masters since he had come into the Northland had bred in him a fear that no master could be permanent. He was afraid that Thornton would pass out of his life as Perrault and François and the Scotch half-breed had passed out. Even in the night, in his dreams, he was haunted by this fear. At such times he would shake off sleep and creep through the chill to the flap of the tent, where he would stand and listen to the sound of his master's breathing.

But in spite of this great love he bore John Thornton,

which seemed to bespeak the soft civilizing influence, the strain of the primitive, which the Northland had aroused in him, remained alive and active. Faithfulness and devotion, things born of fire and roof, were his; yet he retained his wildness and wiliness. He was a thing of the wild, come in from the wild to sit by John Thornton's fire, rather than a dog of the soft Southland stamped with the marks of generations of civilization. Because of his very great love, he could not steal from this man, but from any other man, in any other camp, he did not hesitate an instant; while the cunning with which he stole enabled him to escape detection.

His face and body were scored by the teeth of many dogs, and he fought as fiercely as ever and more shrewdly. Skeet and Nig were too good-natured for quarrelling,—besides, they belonged to John Thornton; but the strange dog, no matter what the breed or valor, swiftly acknowledged Buck's supremacy or found himself struggling for life with a terrible antagonist. And Buck was merciless. He had learned well the law of club and fang, and he never forewent an advantage or drew back from a foe he had started on the way to Death. He had lessoned from Spitz, and from the chief fighting dogs of the police and mail, and knew there was no middle course. He must master or be mastered; while to show mercy was a weakness. Mercy did not exist in the primordial life. It was misunderstood for fear, and such misunderstandings made for death. Kill or be killed, eat or be eaten, was the law; and this mandate, down out of the depths of Time, he obeyed.

He was older than the days he had seen and the breaths he had drawn. He linked the past with the present, and the eternity behind him throbbed through him in a mighty rhythm to which he swayed as the tides and seasons swayed. He sat by John Thornton's fire, a broadbreasted dog, white-fanged and long-furred; but behind him were the shades of all manner of dogs, half-wolves and wild wolves, urgent and prompting, tasting the savor of the meat he ate, thirsting for the water he drank, scenting the wind with him, listening with him and telling him the sounds made by the wild life in the forest, dictating his moods, directing his actions, lying down to sleep with him when he lay down, and dreaming with him and beyond him and becoming themselves the stuff of his dreams.

So peremptorily did these shades beckon him, that each day mankind and the claims of mankind slipped farther from him. Deep in the forest a call was sounding, and as often as he heard this call, mysteriously thrilling and luring, he felt compelled to turn his back upon the fire and the beaten earth around it, and to plunge into the forest, and on and on, he knew not where or why; nor did he wonder where or why, the call sounding imperiously, deep in the forest. But as often as he gained the soft unbroken earth and the green shade, the love for John Thornton drew him back to the fire again.

65

Thornton alone held him. The rest of mankind was as nothing. Chance travellers might praise or pet him; but he was cold under it all, and from a too demonstrative man he would get up and walk away. When Thornton's partners, Hans and Pete, arrived on the long-expected raft, Buck refused to notice them till he learned they were close to Thornton; after that he tolerated them in a passive sort of way, accepting favors from them as though he favored them by accepting. They were of the same large type as Thornton, living close to the earth, thinking simply and seeing clearly; and ere they swung the raft into the big eddy by the saw-mill at Dawson, they understood Buck and his ways, and did not insist upon an intimacy such as obtained with Skeet and Nig.

For Thornton, however, his love seemed to grow and grow. He, alone among men, could put a pack upon Buck's back in the summer travelling. Nothing was too great for Buck to do, when Thornton commanded. One day (they had grub-staked themselves from the proceeds of the raft and left Dawson for the head-waters of the Tanana) the men and dogs were sitting on the crest of a cliff which fell away, straight down, to naked bed-rock three hundred feet below. John Thornton was sitting near the edge, Buck at his shoulder. A thoughtless whim seized Thornton, and he drew the attention of Hans and Pete to the experiment he had in mind. "Jump, Buck!" he commanded, sweeping his arm out and over the chasm. The next instant he was grappling with Buck on the extreme edge, while Hans and Pete were dragging them back into safety.

"It's uncanny," Pete said, after it was over and they had caught their speech.

Thornton shook his head. "No, it is splendid, and it is terrible, too. Do you know, it sometimes makes me afraid."

"I'm not hankering to be the man that lays hands on you while he's around," Pete announced conclusively, nodding his head toward Buck.

"Py Jingo!" was Hans's contribution. "Not mineself either."

It was at Circle City, ere the year was out, that Pete's apprehensions were realized. "Black" Burton, a man evil-tempered and malicious, had been picking a quarrel with a tenderfoot at the bar, when Thornton stepped good-naturedly between. Buck, as was his custom, was lying in a corner, head on paws, watching his master's every action. Burton struck out, without warning, straight from the shoulder. Thornton was sent spinning, and saved himself from falling only by clutching the rail of the bar.

Those who were looking on heard what was neither bark nor yelp, but a something which is best described as a roar, and they saw Buck's body rise up in the air as he left the floor for Burton's throat. The man saved his life by instinctively throwing out his arm, but was hurled backward to the floor with Buck on top of him. Buck loosed his teeth from the flesh of the arm and drove in

67

again for the throat. This time the man succeeded only in partly blocking, and his throat was torn open. Then the crowd was upon Buck, and he was driven off; but while a surgeon checked the bleeding, he prowled up and down, growling furiously, attempting to rush in, and being forced back by an array of hostile clubs. A "miners' meeting," called on the spot, decided that the dog had sufficient provocation, and Buck was discharged. But his reputation was made, and from that day his name spread through every camp in Alaska.

Later on, in the fall of the year, he saved John Thornton's life in quite another fashion. The three partners were lining a long and narrow poling-boat down a bad stretch of rapids on Forty-Mile Creek. Hans and Pete moved along the bank, snubbing with a thin Manila rope from tree to tree, while Thornton remained in the boat, helping its descent by means of a pole, and shouting directions to the shore. Buck, on the bank, worried and anxious, kept abreast of the boat, his eyes never off his master.

At a particularly bad spot, where a ledge of barely submerged rocks jutted out into the river, Hans cast off the rope, and, while Thornton poled the boat out into the stream, ran down the bank with the end in his hand to snub the boat when it had cleared the ledge. This it did, and was flying down-stream in a current as swift as a mill-race, when Hans checked it with the rope and checked too suddenly. The boat flirted over and snubbed

in to the bank bottom up, while Thornton, flung sheer .
out of it, was carried down-stream toward the worst part
of the rapids, a stretch of wild water in which no swimmer
could live.

Buck had sprung in on the instant, and at the end of
three hundred yards, amid a mad swirl of water, he over-
hauled Thornton. When he felt him grasp his tail, Buck
headed for the bank, swimming with all his splendid
strength. But the progress shoreward was slow; the progress down-stream amazingly rapid. From below came the
fatal roaring where the wild current went wilder and was
rent in shreds and spray by the rocks which thrust
through like the teeth an enormous comb. The suck of
the water as it took the beginning of the last steep pitch
was frightful, and Thornton knew that the shore was impossible. He scraped furiously over a rock, bruised across
a second, and struck a third with crushing force. He
clutched its slippery top with both hands, releasing Buck,
and above the roar of the churning water shouted: "Go,
Buck! Go!"

Buck could not hold his own, and swept on down-
stream, struggling desperately, but unable to win back.
When he heard Thornton's command repeated, he partly
reared out of the water, throwing his head high, as
though for a last look, then turned obediently toward the
bank. He swam powerfully and was dragged ashore by
Pete and Hans at the very point where swimming ceased
to be possible and destruction began.

69

They knew that the time a man could cling to a slippery rock in the face of that driving current was a matter of minutes, and they ran as fast as they could up the bank to a point far above where Thornton was hanging on. They attached the line with which they had been snubbing the boat to Buck's neck and shoulders, being careful that it should neither strangle him nor impede his swimming, and launched him into the stream. He struck out boldly, but not straight enough into the stream. He discovered the mistake too late, when Thornton was abreast of him and a bare half-dozen strokes away while he was being carried helplessly past.

Hans promptly snubbed with the rope, as though Buck were a boat. The rope thus tightening on him in the sweep of the current, he was jerked under the surface, and under the surface he remained till his body struck against the bank and he was hauled out. He was half drowned, and Hans and Pete threw themselves upon him, pounding the breath into him and the water out of him. He staggered to his feet and fell down. The faint sound of Thornton's voice came to them, and though they could not make out the words of it, they knew that he was in his extremity. His master's voice acted on Buck like an electric shock. He sprang to his feet and ran up the bank ahead of the men to the point of his previous departure.

Again the rope was attached and he was launched, and again he struck out, but this time straight into the stream. He had miscalculated once, but he would not be guilty of it a second time. Hans paid out the rope, permitting no slack, while Pete kept it clear of coils. Buck held on till he was on a line straight above Thornton; then he turned, and with the speed of an express train headed down upon him. Thornton saw him coming, and, as Buck struck him like a battering ram, with the whole force of the current behind him, he reached up and closed with both arms around the shaggy neck. Hans snubbed the rope around the tree, and Buck and Thornton were jerked under the water. Strangling, suffocating, sometimes one uppermost and sometimes the other, dragging over the jagged bottom, smashing against rocks and snags, they veered in to the bank.

Thornton came to, belly downward and being violently propelled back and forth across a drift log by Hans and Pete. His first glance was for Buck, over whose limp and apparently lifeless body Nig was setting up a howl, while Skeet was licking the wet face and closed eyes. Thornton was himself bruised and battered, and he went carefully over Buck's body, when he had been brought around, finding three broken ribs.

"That settles it," he announced. "We camp right here." And camp they did, till Buck's ribs knitted and he was able to travel.

That winter, at Dawson, Buck performed another exploit, not so heroic, perhaps, but one that put his name many notches higher on the totem-pole of Alaskan fame.

71

This exploit was particularly gratifying to the three men; for they stood in need of the outfit which it furnished, and were enabled to make a long-desired trip into the virgin East, where miners had not yet appeared. It was brought about by a conversation in the Eldorado Saloon, in which men waxed boastful of their favorite dogs. Buck, because of his record, was the target for these men, and Thornton was driven stoutly to defend him. At the end of half an hour one man stated that his dog could start a sled with five hundred pounds and walk off with it; a second bragged six hundred for his dog; and a third seven hundred.

"Pooh! pooh!" said John Thornton. "Buck can start a thousand pounds."

"And break it out? And walk off with it for a hundred yards?" demanded Matthewson, a Bonanza King, he of the seven hundred vaunt.

"And break it out, and walk off with it for a hundred yards," John Thornton said coolly.

"Well," Matthewson said, slowly and deliberately, so that all could hear, "I've got a thousand dollars that says he can't. And there it is." So saying, he slammed a sack of gold dust of the size of a bologna sausage down upon the bar.

Nobody spoke. Thornton's bluff, if bluff it was had been called. He could feel a flush of warm blood creeping up his face. His tongue had tricked him. He did not know whether Buck could start a thousand pounds. Half a ton!

 72

The enormousness of it appalled him. He had great faith in Buck's strength and had often thought him capable of starting such a load; but never, as now, had he faced the possibility of it, the eyes of a dozen men fixed upon him, silent and waiting. Further, he had no thousand dollars; nor had Hans or Pete.

"I've got a sled standing outside now, with twenty fifty-pound sacks of flour on it," Matthewson went on with brutal directness, "so don't let that hinder you."

Thornton did not reply. He did not know what to say. He glanced from face to face in the absent way of a man who has lost the power of thought and is seeking somewhere to find the thing that will start it going again. The face of Jim O'Brien, a Mastodon King and old-time comrade, caught his eyes. It was as a cue to him, seeming to rouse him to do what he would never have dreamed of doing.

"Can you lend me a thousand?" he asked, almost in a whisper.

"Sure," answered O'Brien, thumping down a plethoric sack by the side of Matthewson's. "Though it's little faith I'm having, John, that the beast can do the trick."

The Eldorado emptied its occupants into the street to see the test. The tables were deserted, and the dealers and game-keepers came forth to see the outcome of the wager and to lay odds. Several hundred men, furred and mittened, banked around the sled within easy distance. Matthewson's sled, loaded with a thousand pounds of flour,

73

had been standing for a couple of hours, and in the intense cold (it was sixty below zero) the runners had frozen fast to the hard-packed snow. Men offered odds of two to one that Buck could not budge the sled. A quibble arose concerning the phrase "break out." O'Brien contended it was Thornton's privilege to knock the runners loose, leaving Buck to "break it out" from a dead standstill. Matthewson insisted that the phrase included breaking the runners from the frozen grip of the snow. A majority of the men who had witnessed the making of the bet decided in his favor, whereat the odds went up to three to one against Buck.

There were no takers. Not a man believed him capable of the feat. Thornton had been hurried into the wager, heavy with doubt; and now that he looked at the sled itself, the concrete fact, with the regular team of ten dogs curled up in the snow before it, the more impossible the task appeared. Matthewson waxed jubilant.

"Three to one!" he proclaimed. "I'll lay you another thousand at that figure, Thornton. What d'ye say?"

Thornton's doubt was strong in his face, but his fighting spirit was aroused—the fighting spirit that soars above odds, fails to recognize the impossible, and is deaf to all save the clamor for battle. He called Hans and Pete to him. Their sacks were slim, and with his own the three partners could rake together only two hundred dollars. In the ebb of their fortunes, this sum was their total capital;

yet they laid it unhesitatingly against Matthewson's six hundred.

The team of ten dogs was unhitched, and Buck, with his own harness, was put into the sled. He had caught the contagion of the excitement, and he felt that in some way he must do a great thing for John Thornton. Murmurs of admiration at his splendid appearance went up. He was in perfect condition, without an ounce of superfluous flesh, and the one hundred and fifty pounds that he weighed were so many pounds of grit and virility. His furry coat shone with the sheen of silk. Down the neck and across the shoulders, his mane, in repose as it was, half bristled and seemed to lift with every movement, as though excess of vigor made each particular hair alive and active. The great breast and heavy forelegs were no more than in proportion with the rest of the body, where the muscles showed in tight rolls underneath the skin. Men felt these muscles and proclaimed them hard as iron, and the odds went down to two to one.

"Gad, sir! Gad, sir!" stuttered a member of the latest dynasty, a king of the Skookum Benches. "I offer you eight hundred for him, sir, before the test, sir; eight hundred just as he stands."

Thornton shook his head and stepped to Buck's side.

"You must stand off from him," Matthewson protested. "Free play and plenty of room."

The crowd fell silent; only could be heard the voices of

75

the gamblers vainly offering two to one. Everybody acknowledged Buck a magnificent animal, but twenty fifty-pound sacks of flour bulked too large in their eyes for them to loosen their pouchstrings.

Thornton knelt down by Buck's side. He took his head in his two hands and rested cheek on cheek. He did not playfully shake him, as was his wont, or murmur soft love curses; but he whispered in his ear. "As you love me, Buck. As you love me," was what he whispered. Buck whined with suppressed eagerness.

The crowd was watching curiously. The affair was growing mysterious. It seemed like a conjuration. As Thornton got to his feet, Buck seized his mittened hand between his jaws, pressing in with his teeth and releasing slowly, half reluctantly. It was the answer, in terms, not of speech, but of love. Thornton stepped well back.

"Now, Buck," he said.

Buck tightened the traces, then slacked them for a matter of several inches. It was the way he had learned.

"Gee!" Thornton's voice rang out, sharp in the tense silence.

Buck swung to the right, ending the movement in a plunge that took up the slack and with a sudden jerk arrested his one hundred and fifty pounds. The load quivered, and from under the runners arose a crisp crackling.

"Haw!" Thornton commanded.

Buck duplicated the manoeuvre, this time to the left. The crackling turned into a snapping, the sled pivoting and the runners slipping and grating several inches to the side. The sled was broken out. Men were holding their breaths, intensely unconscious of the fact.

"Now, MUSH!"

Thornton's command cracked out like a pistol-shot. Buck threw himself forward, tightening the traces with a jarring lunge. His whole body was gathered compactly together in the tremendous effort, the muscles writhing and knotting like live things under the silky fur. His great chest was low to the ground, his head forward and down, while his feet were flying like mad, the claws scarring the hard-packed snow in parallel grooves. The sled swayed and trembled, half-started forward. One of his feet slipped, and one man groaned aloud. Then the sled lurched ahead in what appeared a rapid succession of jerks, though it never really came to a dead stop again . . . half an inch . . . an inch . . . two inches . . . The jerks perceptibly diminished; as the sled gained momentum, he caught them up, till it was moving steadily along.

Men gasped and began to breathe again, unaware that for a moment they had ceased to breathe. Thornton was running behind, encouraging Buck with short, cheery words. The distance had been measured off, and as he neared the pile of firewood which marked the end of the hundred yards, a cheer began to grow and grow, which burst into a roar as he passed the firewood and halted at command. Every man was tearing himself loose, even

Matthewson. Hats and mittens were flying in the air. Men were shaking hands, it did not matter with whom, and bubbling over in a general incoherent babel.

But Thornton fell on his knees beside Buck. Head was against head, and he was shaking him back and forth. Those who hurried up heard him cursing Buck, and he cursed him long and fervently, and softly and lovingly.

"Gad, sir! Gad, sir!" spluttered the Skookum Bench king. "I'll give you a thousand for him, sir, a thousand, sir—twelve hundred, sir."

Thornton rose to his feet. His eyes were wet. The tears were streaming frankly down his cheeks. "Sir," he said to the Skookum Bench king, "no sir. You can go to hell, sir. It's the best I can do for you, sir."

Buck seized Thornton's hand in his teeth. Thornton shook him back and forth. As though animated by a common impulse, the onlookers drew back to a respectful distance; nor were they again indiscreet enough to interrupt.

"... As Handsome Does"

by GENEVIEVE TORREY EAMES

The Big 4H tent was bustling with activity. Boys and girls were busy working on their exhibits or talking "shop," or looking over one another's entries with a critical eye. Sandy wandered down one aisle and up the next, with a hot dog in one hand and a coke bottle in the other. Handy walked quietly at his heels, politely ignoring the passers-by who spoke to him or leaned over to pet him.

Sandy stopped to look at Frank's lambs, trim and blocky, with their neat little burlap blankets to protect their wool. Frank was standing on the top rail of the pen, tacking a blue ribbon to the beam overhead.

"Hi, Frank," Sandy said. "I see you did all right."

"Gee, yes. I was kinda surprised, though. I thought my lambs were pretty good, but I never expected to get a first."

This story is from HANDY OF THE TRIPLE S, by Genevieve Torrey Eames

79

"Well, I'm glad. They ought to bring a good price, too. What are you going to do with all that money when you sell them?"

"I'm saving up for a good saddle. By the time my colt's grown up, I'll have a real outfit—just as good as Jean's." He jumped down from the fence and rumpled Handy's ruff with a friendly gesture. "How's my old pal, Handy?" he asked.

"Okay, I guess. Anyway, he doesn't know how to worry. But I'm not feeling so good. I'm scared stiff. I never should have entered him in the trials. Mom and Pop said to wait until next year, and I guess they were right."

"Shucks, he'll do fine. You wait and see."

"They're going to start pretty soon. I wish it was over. Are you going to watch?"

"Sure, I'll be there; I wouldn't miss it for anything. Got to get a pail of water for the lambs first."

Sandy strolled over to the arena. The cattle judge was examining a long line of Hereford steers—the 4H Baby Beef entry. It looked as if he would never get to the end and decide on the winners. His father and Bill Allen were leaning over the rail watching the judging and dis- cussing the points of the various animals. The two men had won the team-roping contest the day before and had tied for second place in calf roping. Now the rodeo events were over and they had nothing to do until the end of the Fair.

80

Sandy slipped past his father, without being seen, and went to the other side of the arena. He knew his father had thought it foolish to enter Handy in the sheep-dog trials, though he hadn't said much at the time. Now, when it was too late, Sandy had a secret, depressing feeling that his parents had been right. Of course they hadn't known what a lot of herding experience Handy had had up there in the mountains; but Sandy wondered now just how much that experience was going to count in the trials. It was one thing to round up a huge flock of sheep, hunting for strays and guarding them from coyotes and other dangers—and another to put three strange, wild sheep thrugh a series of gaps in sections of fence, and finally to pen them in a small enclosure.

He had thought he could teach Handy this part of the work by using the lambs he had bought from Frank, but it hadn't been as easy as he expected. The Lambs were too tame; they followed Sandy every where and they seemed to think Handy was another lamb to play with. They soon learned to make the rounds of all the corral gates as if it were some kind of game, and Handy had no chance to develop any real skill. Sandy was sure the dog would obey directions, and he seemed to understand the system of whistles and hand signals that Sandy tried to repeat as he had seen the herder use them. But he was only a puppy, after all; and how he might do in the arena, in front of all those crowds, with everything strange. . .

81

"Oh, golly," Sandy groaned. "I ought to have my head examined."

The Baby-Beef exhibitors were filing out with their steers, and the ring attendants were setting up the gates for the trials. There were five gates in all, two placed along each side and one in the center of the ring. At one end a small pen was set up, made of four sections of hurdle fencing with the fourth side swinging free at one corner to be used as a gate.

Sandy felt his hands getting cold, though the palms were damp with perspiration.

A group of men had gathered near the gate, each with a dog on a lead. The dogs were of all kinds, large and small; most of them were mongrels, but showed at least a mixture of collie. Handy was the only one that wouldn't have looked out of place in a dog show.

The men looked old, Sandy thought, though he didn't pay much attention to them; as far as he was concerned, nothing mattered except the dogs. Were they better than Handy, he wondered, and how much better?

A gaunt-looking man in faded levis had stepped inside the gate. He wore a short, grizzled beard, and his wrinkled face was the color of an old saddle. His pale blue eyes under their bushy brows were permanently squinted, as if from too much looking at the sun. His small yellow dog stuck close to his heels, and sat down beside him while he waited for the judge to give his instructions. Sandy recognized the dog from the previous year; he was a famous trial winner, and no dog in recent years had been able to beat him. Sandy edged closer to listen to the judge.

The sheep must be driven through the first gate on the right; then through the one in the center; next, the second on the right; and back on the other side in the same order. (Like a big croquet game, Sandy thought.) Then they were to be penned in the little enclosure. The shepherd could wave his arms or a stick or his hat, to direct the dog, but he must not actually help him with the sheep except in penning them. If a gate was skipped or taken out of turn or in the wrong direction, the sheep must be driven back and put through it correctly. Time would be taken from the starting whistle, and anything over fifteen minutes would disqualify.

The man nodded to show he understood, and a small truck backed up to the ring entrance. The attendants let down the tailgate and three big, wild-looking sheep sprang, stiff-legged, down to the ground. The little dog quivered with anticipation and excitement, but he did not move. The sheep made a dash for the other end of the ring; wheeled suddenly and stood looking about, their eyes ablaze with suspicion. The timekeeper pulled out his stopwatch, glanced at the man, and blew his whistle.

The man waved his hand; and the little dog was off like a shot, skirting the edge of the ring and creeping, belly-flat, along the ground as he approached the sheep from the rear. He looked back at his master for orders and then brought the trio on a swift run to the upper end of

83

the ring. Before they knew what they were doing, he had turned them sharply around and headed them through the first gap. In spite of the judge's warning hand, a spatter of applause came from the stands and then died away as the sheep sped toward the second gate on the side. A quick command from the shepherd, and like a flash the dog circled the sheep and the hurdles and stood facing them in the opening. They stopped short and turned, and quietly, gently, the dog eased them back and through the center gate. Again the crowd applauded, and the judge took the microphone to ask for quiet.

Sandy's hands were clenched tightly. He forgot that the little dog was Handy's competitor—forgot everything except the urgent desire to see the little fellow get the best of those sheep. "Come on, boy!" he whispered under his breath.

He sighed with relief when the sheep were penned at last, and cheers went up from the crowd as the announcer gave the time—seven and a half minutes. He looked up to the grandstand; his mother and Susie were there, he knew, but he could not see them. He wondered if they would be cheering for Handy after it was all over. Or would they be feeling sorry for him? He felt as if he couldn't stand there and watch another dog go through that ordeal.

"Come along, Handy," he said, and pushed his way through the crowd.

 84

Handy was number seven—the last dog to compete. They would get off somewhere, away from all the people, until his turn came. They walked up and down behind the grandstand and then went over to the corrals where the sheep for the trials were kept. As the truck brought back each lot from the arena, they were put in a separate pen and a new trio picked from the flock, so that no dog would have the advantage of sheep that were used to the course and even partially accustomed to being herded through the gaps. Sandy looked them over, wondering which ones he'd get. Not that it mattered much; they were all wild and strong-willed, and there was no telling how any of them would act in the ring. For the moment Sandy felt that he hated all sheep and particularly the three that Handy would have to face in a few minutes.

"They're calling for number seven," the truck driver said as the tailgate slammed shut for the last time. "Is that you?"

"Yes, it's me."

"That's some dog you got there," the man added, but Sandy was already hurrying back to the ring.

Somebody in the crowd said "My, what a beauty!" as Handy followed him through the gate, but Sandy was hardly conscious of anything except the sudden dryness of his mouth. He tried a low whistle, but his lips felt stiff and he couldn't make a sound. He licked them hastily

85

and tried again; it was no good. He looked around for Frank. A drink of water might help, if he could only ask for one; but all the faces looked strange. It would sound silly to say, "I can't whistle."

He leaned down and took Handy's head in his two hands.

"Look, old fellow," he said in a small, scared voice. "It's up to you. I'll do the best I can, but you're mostly on your own. Just don't let those darned old sheep get the better of you."

The truck backed in and let out the three sheep. Sandy's hopes vanished as he saw them split up and run in three different directions. Handy was eager to go after them and he looked up inquiringly, but Sandy shook his head. "Steady!" he said; then, as the timekeeper's whistle blew, he added, "Go get 'em!"

Handy seemed to feel this was no time for speed and dash. He trotted to the far end of the ring, rounded up the lone sheep that was there and started it toward its companion near the left-side fence. He hung back until they had come together, and then moved up just enough to keep them going slowly in Sandy's direction. The third sheep came out from its hiding place behind the pen and joined the others when it saw them going by. Without hurrying and yet without a lost moment Handy had gathered the three sheep, and now he looked to Sandy for further orders. Sandy waved him toward the first gate.

The sheep made a little rush and then stopped, slightly to one side of the gap, undecided whether to go through or around the end of the fence. Handy crowded them a little; but they only swerved from side to side, stamping their feet restlessly. One false move and they would separate again, and all the dog's work would have to be done over. Sandy was silent. He wanted to whistle a warning to Handy, the soft, low whistle that meant "Go easy"; but his dry lips couldn't make a sound. Why, oh, why, wouldn't the stupid things go through? Why did Handy have to draw such an ornery lot of sheep, anyway?

For a long moment they wavered on the verge of flight, then Handy reaped the benefit of the herder's strict training. From being left constantly with his sheep, with no human companionship, he seemed to have picked up an uncanny knowledge of sheep nature. He took his eyes from the little group as if he had lost interest in them and, turning partly away, walked slowly through the gap. As if they were hypnotized, the sheep followed him.

The crowd broke into a roar and the announcer called, "Quiet, please! Give the dog a chance!"

Sandy breathed again as he pointed toward the center gate, and Handy had the dazed sheep through it and headed for the next one before they could make up their minds to resist. At the third opening they made another stand, but this time the dog did not give them time to refuse. He shouldered the rear sheep until it pushed the others, and all three went through together. He

87

seemed to know instinctively that the longer the bunch kept together the less likely they were to break, and the faster he could drive them.

"Boy, oh, boy! He sure knows his business," Sandy exclaimed.

He had lost all track of time, but so far, at least, he felt confident that Handy could finish within the allotted fifteen minutes. Still, a lot could happen before the sheep were safely penned.

Handy fought, coaxed, and bullied the stubborn little animals through the next three gates. Now there was only the penning, and with luck. . .

Sandy held the fence section with one hand, ready to shut it the moment the sheep were safely inside. But here Handy's luck seemed to desert him. One sheep went into the pen, but the other two veered off at the last moment and ran around the outside. Sandy couldn't keep the one sheep in and still hold the gate open for the others, so he let it go.

Handy rounded them up and made a second try, but this time all three made a break for the other end of the arena. Before they had gone halfway, Handy headed them off and turned them back toward the pen. This time he brought them very slowly, keeping them closely bunched.

"Easy, boy, easy!" Sandy was saying, but more to himself than to the dog. The sheep were only a few feet away now, and staring at the boy as if he were some strange

 88

animal. Sandy, clutching the gate with his left hand and holding his right arm out so the sheep wouldn't pass him on that side, hardly dared to blink for fear of starting a stampede. Handy moved up on the outside and made a sudden rush, taking the sheep by surprise. They dashed into the pen and turned to escape, but Sandy had slammed the gate shut and was holding it tight with both hands.

Sandy hardly knew what happened next; people crowded around, the judge made an announcement over the loudspeaker, and Susie appeared from somewhere and threw her arms around Handy's neck.

"Tough luck!" he heard Frank say.

"What's tough about it?" Sandy asked. "He made it, didn't he? He wasn't disqualified?"

"Didn't you hear the judge announce the time? Eight minutes, flat. With a little more luck at the end, he'd have been first."

"You mean he's second? No kidding? Golly catfish, it seemed like hours."

Then a hard, bony hand was shaking his, and he looked up into the smiling face of the old-timer who had run the first dog.

"That feller don't know what luck is," the old man was saying. "With that ornery bunch of critters you was lucky they didn't all jump the fence and take to the hills. But it was good work, son; I don't believe my Shep could have handled 'em any better. If you're aimin' to enter again

89

next year, I figger I better retire the old boy while he's ahead."

Then there were photographers taking pictures of the two dogs and their owners, and at last the crowd thinned out and the ring was cleared for the next event.

Sandy left Handy with his mother and Susie.

"Wait for me, Mom," he said. "I've got to see Pop."

He met his father working his way through the crowd around the arena.

"That was swell, son," Sam said. "I was surprised, too. I knew you'd been working on the pup, but I never thought you'd get far in such a short time."

"Oh, that!" Sandy said. "I didn't teach him much. He learned most of it from that old herder up in the mountains. You know, I'm glad now he was lost so long. He sure learned to know sheep."

"Well, wherever he learned it, he's as good a dog as I'd want to see."

This, from Sam, was high praise; but there was one thing more.

"Say, Pop, do you remember that old saying of your grandmother's—that one about 'Handsome is as handsome does'? Well, don't you think Handy 'does' and 'is' too?"

"Listen, son; I think he 'does' and 'is' the best dog in California. And if anybody doubts it, you just send them to me!"

Sandy's face broke into a grin. "That's all I wanted to

 90

know," he said. "Be seein' you; I gotta go buy Handy a hot dog."

Always Reddy

by MARGUERITE HENRY

. . . . . Something far more serious was happening to Reddy. It seemed every now and then as if her legs were not her own. They refused to obey her will.

Mornings when she wanted to dance on her hind feet and plant her forepaws on Mr. Hoops' shoulders, she could not make it.

It was worse on a morning after a hard workout in the field, especially if the weather had been frosty and the birds had fallen in water. One morning she felt so stiff and sore that she could not get up until the sun found her bed and toasted her bones. Then, gradually, she limbered up and by noon she seemed as good as ever.

It was strange that Mr. Hoops suspected nothing. If Reddy failed to race and tear about the basement when he arrived, he laid it to sleepiness.

"Why, you lazy old girl!" he would say. "Pretty soft to lie abed all hours."

Then Reddy would make a great effort to rise.

This story is from ALWAYS REDDY, by Marguerite Henry

"I declare!" Mr. Hoops would laugh. "You're as stilty-legged as a colt."

On dry sunny days, however, Reddy seemed livelier than ever before. She could put her paws clear up on Mr. Hoops' shoulders with no trouble at all. And she was so glad about it that she gave his ears and neck an extra good licking.

All through the hunting season Snippet gained in skill while Reddy seemed to let down, but Mr. Hoops admitted this to no one. He scarcely admitted it to himself. What if Reddy did not range out as wide as Snippet? What if she seemed to avoid fences and hedgerows? She still had a sure nose for birds and pointed them like an arrow.

One day several birds that Mr. Hoops hit fell into a creek swollen by fall rains. He watched amazed as Reddy just stood on the bank and let Snippet retrieve them. She made no move to help him.

Mr. Hoops had to call her name out sharply before she finally splashed her way into the water and did her share of the work. Even then Mr. Hoops did not suspect.

It was the last day of the hunting season before Mr. Hoops knew.

The weather was unpromising. In spite of a crust of snow on the ground, the air was dry with a wind so fierce that it scattered all bird scent. As Snippet dashed over the rough country, Reddy seemed almost to crouch along. Mr. Hoops wondered if rheumatism had at last caught up with her, but he closed the little shutters of his mind.

93

"She's just smart," he told himself. "Saving her strength for a real burst of speed when she needs it."

The day wore itself out. By twilight Mr. Hoops' game-bag was still empty. "I know we should be getting home," he told Reddy and Snippet, "but I always like to take at least one bird to Mrs. Hoops. What do you say to working the alder thicket once more? The wind seems to be dying a little. Our luck is bound to change."

Snippet wagged his tail in agreement and Reddy seemed more eager than when they had started out. It was almost as if she knew that this was the last hour of the hunting season.

At a wave of the hat both dogs made a beeline for the alder thicket. Now Snippet was clearing a split rail fence. But Reddy! She was not going to clear it. Mr. Hoops watched horrified as she hit the top rail, was catapulted into the air, and then fell in a little heap in the leaves.

It was only a matter of seconds until he reached the spot where she lay, but to him it seemed hours. Snippet had already found her, and when Mr. Hoops reached them he was licking a tiny trickle of blood on her forehead.

He dropped to his knees beside Reddy and pillowed her head in his lap. "She tried to tell me in the only way she knew. Please, God," he prayed, "don't let her die."

He glanced about helplessly. The ground was hummocky, but between the hummocks were pockets of snow. With quick hands he filled his handkerchief with the snow and placed it on Reddy's head. She made no move then nor when he felt of her legs to see if they were broken. He listened to her breathing but could hardly hear it for his own.

"Reddy," he pleaded, "if you'll get well, we'll have the best of days together. I'll rub your legs with warm liniment night and morning. You'll never have to work the fields again. And when spring comes you can lie on a warm rug in the sun and watch me plant my garden. Why, you can sleep all day if you like!"

He took off his jacket and wrapped it closely about her. How quiet the world seemed! A squirrel came to look at them with an inquiring glance, but did not even scold.

Night was closing in when Mr. Hoops felt a stirring in his arms. He pressed his ear against Reddy's muzzle to hear any faint cries of pain. There was none. Reddy was opening her eyes. She was trying to lick Mr. Hoops' face. She was trying to comfort *him!*

Joyously Mr. Hoops carried his precious burden to the car. Then he sped for the warmth of the City Hall.

"Reddy's had an accident," he told Mrs. Hoops over the telephone. "I'll spend the night here. Yes, Hannah, there's a cot to sleep on. I'll be all right."

It was long past midnight before Mr. Hoops slept. He sponged the blood from Reddy's head and cut away some of her matted hair. He bathed the wound with flowers

95

of sulphur. Then he wrapped her in his old hunting coat and placed her near the furnace. She fell into a fitful sleep while he and Snippet looked on.

Mr. Hoops could not help noticing how Snippet had changed. In just a few hours he had grown from a playful youngster into a responsible dog. It was as if he were the parent now and Reddy the overgrown pup to be watched over.

"Snippet," said Mr. Hoops softly, "it's time you had your supper. Nothing fancy tonight. Just dry crumbles moistened with beef tea."

While Snippet cleaned his bowl, Mr. Hoops heated some milk, beat an egg into it, and added a little beef tea. Then, very gently, he lifted Reddy's jowl and poured a teaspoonful of the warm liquid between her teeth. She swallowed it and then ever so faintly began to whimper. She could stand the scratch of briers and the thwack of a fence rail, but when the master bent low over her in sympathy she cried.

Now Mr. Hoops moistened his finger in the liquid and let Reddy lick it as if she were a puppy. And soon she was lapping the milk not because she wanted it, but because it seemed to please him.

When she could drink no more, Mr. Hoops examined her carefully. Besides the gash on her head, the pads of her feet were cut by splinters and thorns.

She seemed very tired now, so Mr. Hoops covered her and let her sleep.

96

Meanwhile he made a table out of a barrel and spread open his dog emergency kit. With skilled fingers he cut and sewed four boots out of white leather. He made them long enough to fit well above Reddy's knees. Then he lined the insides of them with a layer of balsam salve and set them on top of the furnace to warm.

At midnight Reddy woke with a whining cry. She was ashamed of it immediately afterward, for she licked Mr. Hoops' hands as he took out the splinters and the thorns from the feathering between her toes. At last he fitted her paws into the boots he had made and covered her again with his coat. In a very few minutes she began to snore.

With a deep sigh, Mr. Hoops tiptoed upstairs to finish the night on the Mayor's cot.

Reddy's wounds healed like magic. Even her morning lameness improved now that she spent most of her time indoors where it was warm and dry. She could climb stairs as well as ever, and she could dance on her hind feet when she had a mind to. But in spite of all this, she was not happy.

All her life she had been a worker. As long as she could remember she had worked the fields for Mr. Hoops or helped him in the training of her puppies. And the harder she worked, the happier she had been.

Now, all that was over. No one needed her, not even Snippet. She had nothing to do. And the days stumbled over each other endlessly.

97

Meanwhile, things began to go wrong at the City Hall. It wasn't anything big or important that happened. Just little things that added up to something big.

The high school band began to practice on the second floor of the City Hall, and every time the tuba hit a certain note Reddy and Snippet howled uncontrollably. It put the Mayor and Bessie, and even the four Commissioners, on edge.

Then Victoria had kittens in the coal room, and if either dog so much as passed her door, she leaped out like a tigress and clawed at them until the yelping was dreadful to hear.

On top of all this Reddy hunted in her dreams. Sometimes she found pheasant and partridge and quail. Then she would bark with joy. More often, however, she failed to jump over a fence, and moaned in a way that was half-human.

But the final incident that brought in a score of complaints was when Snippet got his nose caught in a mousetrap. He let out such a bloodcurdling cry that a woman customer at Mr. Hoops' window fell to the floor in a faint.

"Adam," said the mayor as kindly as he could, "the time has come to find a kennel for your dogs." Then at an imploring look from Katy he added, "Of course, you can wait for slightly warmer days."

Mr. Hoops was a man who never went to meet trouble.

98

He waited for it to catch up with him and tap him on the shoulder. Sometimes he even waited until it whirled him about sharply.

"Time enough," he said to Reddy and Snippet one Saturday night soon after the mousetrap incident, "time enough to think about leaving here when warm weather comes. We got through yesterday, didn't we? All right, we'll get through tomorrow too. You'll see."

And he tried to whistle a gay tune as he stirred a pot of mulligan. But every now and then the whistling stopped and was a long time starting up again.

During one of these pauses, Officer O'Toole rattled the front door. Mr. Hoops let him in and invited him downstairs to sit awhile.

"Don't offer me any of that mulligatawny, Adam. I could clean the whole pot, and what would the dogs think if I did the like of that? It smells elegant!" he sniffed.

Mr. Hoops laughed. "Occasionally I sample it myself, but I always feel like a dog when I do."

Reddy and Snippet rubbed against the officer's legs.

"It was the Mayor sent me," Officer O'Toole said, as he bent over to pat the dogs. "He stops me as he drives by and says, 'O'Toole, would you be so kind as to drop in on Adam and tell him to be sure the safe is locked? I put some mighty important papers in it, O'Toole,' he says, 'and I can't remember for the life of me whether I locked it or not. 'Twould worry me all Sunday,' he says.

99

"Then I gives him the green light and away he goes," chuckled the policeman. "And now I've got to skedaddle too."

Mr. Hoops saw Officer O'Toole to the door. Then he tried the handle of the safe which he had locked when the five-o'clock whistle blew. This was a firm habit with Mr. Hoops. He felt more responsibility for the city's money and papers than if they had been his own. Only the City Treasurer and the Mayor knew the combination of this safe.

With a little sigh of relief at the peace and quiet, he began to jot down all of the things he wanted to do on Monday. At the very bottom of the list he wrote hurriedly, "Look up a good kennel man." He penciled this last quite faintly, almost as if he thought that the words and the need for them might vanish over the week end.

When, that same evening, Mrs. Hoops saw Mr. Hoops come home without his hat, she knew that he was worried over something. Quite rightly, she suspected it concerned Reddy and Snippet.

And then Mrs. Hoops said something which gave Mr. Hoops a jolt. "Just because Reddy's hunting days are over," she remarked, "just because of that is no reason Snippet should be neglected. Don't you think you should be hardening him so he'll be in condition for the hunting season?"

Mr. Hoops looked at Mrs. Hoops in wonderment.

100

Every now and again she would come out with a suggestion that showed she understood dogs too.

So it was that on the following day, which was Sunday, Mr. Hoops took Snippet out alone. Before they set off together he stooped down and had a word with Reddy. Then with his eyes carefully avoiding hers, he smoothed her head and said good-by.

Reddy made no move to follow. Yet she seemed to believe they could not really go off without her, for she stood up now, waiting to be invited.

As Snippet bounded up the stairs after Mr. Hoops, Reddy scarcely breathed. She heard the sound of their footfalls along the corridor. She heard the door to the street close with a terrible finality. She ran over to the window to hear her name, no matter how softly it might be called. But no voice came. Mr. Hoops' footsteps were growing fainter now, and the click of Snippet's toenails on the sidewalk could no longer be heard at all. She gave one loud bark as a reminder to them, but the only answer was her own echo. So she stood there for a long time nosing the air coming in through the window. She could smell spring, and a great longing filled her.

With Snippet gone, the basement suddenly seemed hushed and chill. The ticking of the clock on the wall upstairs only emphasized the quiet.

Reddy walked slowly to her rug, but she was restless and could not sleep. Trembling a little, she got up and

101

made her way to the coal room. Even a scuffle with Victoria and her kittens was to be preferred to all this stillness. But a sniff around the coal room revealed that Victoria and her entire family had gone out too. Miserably, Reddy returned to her own quarters.

Minute after minute ticked by. Finally, with a sigh of weariness, she flopped down on her rug. She had almost fallen asleep when suddenly she twitched and was wide awake. The door upstairs was opening. Then it clicked shut, quietly and quickly. A stranger was walking overhead with hurried steps.

Reddy was alert at once. She crept cautiously up the stairs, her hackles rising. Unmindful of any danger to herself she went into Mr. Hoops' office. A man stood close to the safe, his back toward Reddy. Quietly she circled him, her nose reaching out to sift his scent from the familiar belongings of Mr. Hoops.

Instinctively she disliked him and let out a low warning growl. The man wheeled about, reaching for his gun. Then with frightening quickness he began beating at Reddy with the butt end of it. The hard steel hit her, now on the shoulders, now on the flanks. Yet the shock of the blows did not confuse her thinking. It whipped her into a fury of strength. She hurled herself at the prowler with such force that he was thrown against the wall.

And to a crash of glass and brass and bells that frightened Reddy more than the blows of the gun, the wall

102

clock came bumping down on the thief's head. With a heavy thud, he fell to the floor.

The clock was in ruins. Coiled springs, wheels, pinions, and the big shiny pendulum were spilled over the thief's chest, and the hour hand was stuck through his hair. It gave him a rakish look.

Reddy stood there puzzled. She was covered with fine splinters of glass, but none had penetrated her coat. She shook herself, stepped carefully over the glass and wire, and made her way to the man. He lay very still.

She stood guard over him. Her shoulders ached from the blows, but she did not mind the pain at all. At last she had work to do. She must hold this stranger until her master returned. Steady. Steady. He would come.

How still everything seemed! Even the ticking noise had stopped. Outside, a Sunday quiet hung over the street. Only a few sparrows were making twittering remarks to each other. The prowler groaned, but made no move.

Finally the streets began to liven with men and women and children coming home from church. But Reddy never wavered. Even when the lock turned, she stood rigid, though she knew in a flash that it was Mr. Hoops and Snippet.

Anxious to see how Reddy fared, Mr. Hoops walked hurriedly down the corridor. He gave only a passing glance into his office, but that was enough to show him the opened safe, and the thief with Reddy on guard.

103

At that very instant, the thief opened his eyes, but when he saw two red dogs where before he had seen only one, he closed them quickly again.

"Steady, Partner! Steady!" breathed Mr. Hoops. He reached for the telephone and called Officer O'Toole and the Mayor. Officer O'Toole came running, his dinner napkin still stuffed between his brass buttons. Close on his heels followed the Mayor and two of the four Commissioners.

There was such a hubbub in the crowded cage that Mr. Hoops and his dogs slipped downstairs unnoticed.

Reddy gave one glad cry when she and Snippet and Mr. Hoops were back together again. She began to leap and run in circles around Mr. Hoops, and there was an air of importance in the very way she wagged her tail. It reminded him of the way she used to act after a good day of hunting when things had gone just right.

Upstairs, Mayor Twitterton was saying to the Policeman O'Toole, "I'm sorry I asked Adam to move his dogs out. Reddy has done the citizens of Belleville a great service today. I had no idea that the City Hall needed a watchdog. So long as I am Mayor, she and her pup shall live right here in City Hall."

And since he had already been Mayor for a dozen years, and since his campaign for Congress was not going along too well, it looked as if he would go right on being Mayor for another dozen years.

104

With the thief handcuffed and the two Commissioners on watch, the Mayor and Policeman O'Toole went downstairs to break the good news to Mr. Hoops.

But they got only as far as the landing. There they stopped suddenly, realizing that he must have overheard the Mayor's announcement.

"Did you hear that? Everything's going to be all right," Mr. Hoops was telling Reddy. "Snippet can take over the field work, and you have a new job guarding City Hall." Then a look of triumph crossed his face. "Why, you've got about the most important job in all Belleville!"

Too happy to say more, he swooped the great gangling dog into his arms and danced a funny little jig, in and out among Katy's mops and pails.

105

Gulliver The Great

WALTER A. DYER

It was a mild evening in early spring, and the magnolias
were in bloom. We motored around the park, turned up
a side street, and finally came to a throbbing standstill
before the Churchwarden Club.

There was nothing about its exterior to indicate that it
was a clubhouse at all, but within there was an indefin-
able atmosphere of early Victorian comfort. There was
something about it that suggested Mr. Pickwick. Old
prints of horses and ships and battles hung upon the
walls, and the oak was dark and old. There seemed to be
no decorative scheme or keynote, and yet the atmosphere was utterly distinctive. It was my first visit to the
Churchwarden Club, of which my quaint, old-fashioned
Uncle Ford had long been a member, and I was charmed.

We dined in the rathskeller, the walls of which were
completely covered with long churchwarden pipes, arranged in the most intricate and marvelous patterns;

This story is from GULLIVER THE GREAT, by Walter A. Dyer

and after our mutton-chop and ale and plum pudding, we filled with the choicest of tobaccos the pipes which the old major-domo brought us.

Then came Jacob R. Enderby to smoke with us.

Tall and spare he was, with long, straight, black hair, large, aquiline nose, and piercing eyes. I disgraced myself by staring at him. I didn't know such a man existed in New York, and yet I couldn't decide whether his habitat should be Arizona or Cape Cod.

Enderby and Uncle Ford were deep in a discussion of the statesmanship of James G. Blaine, when a waiter summoned my uncle to the telephone.

I neglected to state that my uncle, in his prosaic hours, is a physician; and this was a call. I knew it the moment I saw the waiter approaching. I was disappointed and disgusted.

Uncle Ford saw this and laughed.

"Cheer up!" said he. "You needn't come with me to visit the sick. I'll be back in an hour, and meanwhile Mr. Enderby will take care of you; won't you, Jake?"

For answer Enderby arose, and refilling his pipe took me by the arm, while my uncle got into his overcoat. As he passed us on the way out he whispered in my ear:

"Talk about dogs."

I heard and nodded.

Enderby led me to the lounge or loafing-room, an oak-paneled apartment in the rear of the floor above, with

107

huge leather chairs and a seat in the bay window. Save for a gray-haired old chap dozing over a copy of Simplicissimus, the room was deserted.

But no sooner had Enderby seated himself on the window-seat than there was a rush and a commotion, and a short, glad bark, and Nubbins, the steward's bull-terrier, bounded in and landed at Enderby's side with canine expressions of great joy.

I reached forward to pat him, but he paid absolutely no attention to me.

At last wrigglings subsided, and he settled down with his head on Enderby's knee, the picture of content. Then I recalled my Uncle's parting injunction.

"Friend of yours?" I suggested.

Enderby smiled. "Yes," he said, "we're friends, I guess. And the funny part of it is that he doesn't pay any attention to any one else except his master. They all act that way with me, dogs do." And he pulled Nubbins's stubby ears.

"Natural attraction, I suppose," said I.

"Yes, it is," he answered, with the modest frankness of a big man. "It's a thing hard to explain, though there's a sort of reason for it in my case."

I pushed toward him a little tobacco-laden teak-wood stand hopefully. He refilled and lighted.

"It's an extraordinary thing, even so," he said, puffing. "Every dog nowadays seems to look upon me as his long-lost master, but it wasn't always so. I hated dogs and they hated me."

Not wishing to say "Really" or "Indeed" to this big, outdoor man, I simply grunted my surprise.

"Yes, we were born enemies. More than that, I was afraid of dogs. A little fuzzy toy dog, ambling up to me in a room full of company, with his tail wagging, gave me the shudders. I couldn't touch the beast. And as for big dogs outdoors, I feared them like the plague. I would go blocks out of my way to avoid one.

"I don't remember being particularly cowardly about other things, but I just couldn't help this. It was in my blood, for some reason or other. It was the bane of my existence. I couldn't see what the brutes were put in the world for, or how any one could have anything to do with them.

"All the dogs reciprocated. They disliked and distrusted me. The most docile old Brunos would growl and show their teeth when I came near."

"Did the change come suddenly?" I asked.

"Quite. It was in 1901. I accepted a commission from an importing and trading company to go to the Philippines to do a little quiet exploring, and spent four months in the sickly place. Then I got the fever, and when I recovered I couldn't get out of there too soon.

"I reached Manila just in time to see the mail steamer disappearing around the point, and I was mad. There

109

would be another in six days, but I couldn't wait. I was just crazy to get back home.

"I made inquiries and learned of an old tramp steamer, named the Old Squaw, making ready to leave for Honolulu on the following day with a cargo of hemp and stuff, and a bunch of Moros for some show in the States, and I booked passage on that.

"She was the worst old tub you ever saw. I didn't learn much about her, but I verily believe her to have been a condemned excursion boat. She wouldn't have been allowed to run to Coney Island.

"She was battered and unpainted, and she wallowed horribly. I don't believe she could have reached Honolulu much before the regular boat, but I couldn't wait, and I took her.

"I made myself as comfortable as possible, bribed the cook to insure myself against starvation, and swung a hammock on the forward deck as far as possible from the worst of the vile smells.

"But we hadn't lost sight of Manila Bay when I discovered that there was a dog aboard—and such a dog! I had never seen one that sent me into such a panic as this one, and he had free range of the ship. A Great Dane he was, named Gulliver, and he was the pride of the captain's rum-soaked heart.

"With all my fear, I realized he was a magnificent animal, but I looked on him as a gigantic devil. Without exception, he was the biggest dog I ever saw, and as muscu-

110

lar as a lion. He lacked some points that show-judges set store by, but he had the size and the build. cop. 5

"I had seen Vohl's Vulcan and the Wurttemberg breed, but they were fox-terriers compared with Gulliver. His tail was as big around as my arm, and the cook lived in terror of his getting into the galley and wagging it; and he had a mouth that looked to me like the crater of Mauna Loa, and a voice that shook the planking when he spoke.

"I first caught sight of him appearing from behind a huge coil of cordage in the stern. He stretched and yawned, and I nearly died of fright.

"I caught up a belaying-pin, though little good that would have done me. I think he saw me do it, and doubtless he set me down for an enemy then and there.

"We were well out of the harbor, and there was no turning back, but I would have given my right hand to be off that boat. I fully expected him to eat me up, and I slept with that belaying-pin sticking into my ribs in the hammock, and with my revolver loaded and handy.

"Fortunately, Gulliver's dislike for me took the form of sublime contempt. He knew I was afraid of him, and he despised me for it. He was a great pet with the captain and crew, and even the Moros treated him with admiring respect when they were allowed on deck. I couldn't understand it. I would as soon have made a pet of a hungry boa-constrictor.

"On the third day out the poor old boiler burst and

111

the Old Squaw caught fire. She was dry and rotten inside and she burned like tinder. No attempt was made to extinguish the flames, which got into the hemp in the hold in short order.

"The smoke was stifling, and in a jiffy all hands were struggling with the boats. The Moros came tumbling up from below and added to the confusion with their terrified yells.

"The davits were old and rusty, and the men were soon fighting among themselves. One boat dropped stern foremost, filled, and sank immediately, and the Old Squaw herself was visibly settling.

"I saw there was no chance of getting away in the boats, and I recalled a life-raft on the deck forward near my hammock. It was a sort of catamaran—a double platform on a pair of hollow, water-tight, cylindrical buoys. It wasn't twenty feet long and about half as broad, but it would have to do. I fancy it was a forgotten relic of the old excursion-boat days.

"There was no time to lose, for the Old Squaw was bound to sink presently. Besides, I was aft with the rest, and the flames were licking up the deck and running-gear in the waist of the boat.

"The galley, which was amidships near the engine-room, had received the full force of the explosion, and the cook lay moaning in the lee scuppers with a small water-cask thumping against his chest. I couldn't stop to help the man, but I did kick the cask away.

 112

"It seemed to be nearly full, and it occurred to me that I should need it. I glanced quickly around, and luckily found a tin of biscuits that had also been blown out of the galley. I picked this up, and rolling the cask of water ahead of me as rapidly as I could, I made my way through the hot, stifling smoke to the bow of the boat.

"I kicked at the life-raft; it seemed to be sound, and I lashed the biscuits and water to it. I also threw on a coil of rope and a piece of sail-cloth. I saw nothing else about that could possibly be of any value to me. I abandoned my trunk for fear it would only prove troublesome.

"Then I hacked the raft loose with my knife and shoved it over the bulwark. Apparently no one had seen me, for there was no one else forward of the sheet of flame that now cut the board in two.

"The raft was a mighty heavy affair, but I managed to raise one end to the rail. I don't believe I would ever have been able to heave it over under any circumstances, but I didn't have to.

"I felt a great unheaval, and the prow of the Old Squaw went up into the air. I grabbed the ropes that I had lashed the food on with and clung to the raft. The deck became almost perpendicular, and it was a miracle that the raft didn't slide down with me into the flames. Somehow it stuck where it was.

"Then the boat sank with a great roar, and for about a thousand years, it seemed to me, I was under water. I didn't do anything, I couldn't think.

113

"I was only conscious of tremendous weight of water and a feeling that I would burst open. Instinct alone made me cling to the raft.

"When it finally brought me to the surface I was as nearly dead as I care to be. I lay there on the thing in a half-conscious condition for an endless time. If my life had depended on my doing something, I would have been lost.

"Then gradually I came to, and began to spit out salt water and gasp for breath. I gathered my wits together and sat up. My hands were absolutely numb, and I had to loosen the grip of my fingers with the help of my toes. Odd sensation.

"Then I looked about me. My biscuits and water and rope were safe, but the sail-cloth had vanished. I remember that this annoyed me hugely at the time, though I don't know what earthly good it would have been.

"The sea was fairly calm, and I could see all about. Not a human being was visible, only a few floating bits of wreckage. Every man on board must have gone down with the ship and drowned, except myself.

"Then I caught sight of something that made my heart stand still. The huge head of Gulliver was coming rapidly toward me through the water!

"The dog was swimming strongly, and must have leaped from the Old Squaw before she sank. My raft was the only thing afloat large enough to hold him, and he knew it.

114

He heaved his huge bulk over the edge

"I drew my revolver, but it was soaking wet and useless. Then I sat down on the cracker tin and gritted my teeth and waited. I had been alarmed, I must admit, when the boiler blew up and the panic began, but that was nothing to the terror that seized me now.

"Here I was all alone on the top of the Pacific Ocean with a horrible demon making for me as fast as he could swim. My mind was benumbed, and I could think of nothing to do. I trembled and my teeth rattled. I prayed for a shark, but no shark came.

"Soon Gulliver reached the raft and placed one of his forepaws on it and then the other. The top of it stood six or eight inches above the water, and it took a great effort for the dog to raise himself. I wanted to kick him back, but I didn't dare to move.

"Gulliver struggled mightily. Again and again he reared his great shoulders above the sea, only to be cast back scratching and kicking, at a lurch of the raft.

"Finally a wave favored him, and he caught the edge of the under platform with one of his hind feet. With a stupendous effort he heaved his huge bulk over the edge and lay sprawling at my feet, panting and trembling."

Enderby paused and gazed out of the window with a big sigh, as though the recital of his story had brought back some of the horror of his remarkable experience.

Nubbins looked up inquiringly, and then snuggled closer to his friend, while Enderby smoothed the white head.

116

"Well," he continued, "there we were. You can't possibly imagine how I felt unless you, too, have been afflicted with dog-fear. It was awful. And I hated the brute so. I could have torn him limb from limb if I had had the strength. But he was vastly more powerful than I. I could only fear him.

"By and by he got up and shook himself. I cowered on my cracker-tin, but he only looked at me contemptuously, went to the other end of the raft, and lay down to wait patiently for deliverance.

"We remained this way until nightfall. The sea was comparatively calm, and we seemed to be drifting but slowly. We were in the path of ships likely to be passing one way or the other, and I would have been hopeful of the outcome if it had not been for my feared and hated companion.

"I began to feel faint, and opened the cracker-tin. The biscuits were wet with salt water, but I ate a couple, and left the tin open to dry them. Gulliver looked around, and I shut the tin hastily. But the dog never moved. He was not disposed to ask any favors. By kicking the sides of the cask and prying with my knife, I managed to get the bung out and took a drink. Then I settled myself on the raft with my back against the cask, and longed for a smoke.

"The gentle motion of the raft produced a lulling effect on my exhausted nerves, and I began to nod, only to awake with a start, with fear gripping at my heart. I

117

dared not sleep. I don't know what I thought Gulliver would do to me, for I did not understand dogs, but I felt that I must watch him constantly. In the star-light I could see that his eyes were open. Gulliver was watchful too.

"All night long I kept up a running fight with drowsiness. I dozed at intervals, but never for long at a time. It was a horrible night, and I cannot tell you how I longed for day and welcomed it when it came.

"I must have slept toward dawn, for I suddenly became conscious of broad daylight. I roused myself, stood up, and swung my arms and legs to stir up circulation, for the night had been chilly. Gulliver arose, too, and stood silently watching me until I ceased for fear. When he had settled down again I got my breakfast out of the cracker-tin. Gulliver was restless, and was evidently interested.

" 'He must be hungry,' I thought, and then a new fear caught me. I had only to wait until he became very hungry and then he would surely attack me. I concluded that it would be wiser to feed him, and I tossed him a biscuit.

"I expected to see him grab it ravenously, and wondered as soon as I had thrown it if the taste of food would only serve to make him more ferocious. But at first he would not touch it. He only lay there with his great head on his paws and glowered at me. Distrust was plainly visible in his face. I had never realized before that a dog's face could express the subtler emotions.

118

"His gaze fascinated me, and I could not take my eyes from his. The bulk of him was tremendous as he lay there, and I noticed the big, swelling muscles of his jaw. At last he arose, sniffed suspiciously at the biscuit, and looked up at me again.

" 'It's all right; eat it!' I cried.

"The sound of my own voice frightened me. I had not intended to speak to him. But in spite of my strained tone he seemed somewhat reassured.

"He took a little nibble, and then swallowed the biscuit after one or two crunches, and looked up expectantly. I threw him another and he ate that.

" 'That's all,' said I. 'We must be sparing of them.'

"I was amazed to discover how perfectly he understood. He lay down again and licked his chops.

"Late in the afternoon I saw a line of smoke on the horizon, and saw a steamer stove into view. I stood up and waved my coat frantically, but to no purpose. Gulliver stood up and looked from me to the steamer, apparently much interested.

" 'Too far off,' I said to Gulliver. 'I hope the next one will come nearer.'

"At midday I dined, and fed Gulliver. This time he took the two biscuits quite without reserve and whacked his great tail against the raft. It seemed to me that his attitude was less hostile, and I wondered at it.

"When I took my drink from the cask, Gulliver showed signs of interest.

119

" 'I suppose dogs get thirsty, too,' I said aloud.

"Gulliver rapped with his tail. I looked about for some sort of receptacle, and finally pulled off my shoe, filled it with water, and shoved it toward him with my foot. He drank gratefully.

"During the afternoon I sighted another ship, but it was too distant to notice me. However, the sea remained calm and I did not despair.

"After we had had supper, I settled back against my cask, resolved to keep awake, for still I did not trust Gulliver. The sun set suddenly and the stars came out, and I found myself strangely lonesome. It seemed as though I had been alone out there on the Pacific for weeks. The miles and miles of heaving waters, almost on a level with my eye, were beginning to get on my nerves. I longed for someone to talk to, and wished I had dragged the half-breed cook along with me for company. I sighed loudly, and Gulliver raised his head.

" 'Lonesome out here, isn't it?' I said, simply to hear the sound of my own voice.

"Then for the first time Gulliver spoke. He made a deep sound in his throat, but it wasn't a growl, and with all my ignorance of dog language I knew it.

"Then I began to talk. I talked about everything—the people back home and all that—and Gulliver listened. I know more about dogs now, and I know that the best way to make friends with a dog is to talk to him. He can't

120

talk back, but he can understand a heap more than you think he can.

"Finally Gulliver, who had kept his distance all this time, arose and came toward me. My words died in my throat. What was he going to do? To my immense relief he did nothing but sink down at my feet with a grunt and curl his huge body into a semicircle. He had dignity, Gulliver had. He wanted to be friendly, but he would not presume. However, I had lost interest in conversation, and sat watching him and wondering.

"In spite of my firm resolution, I fell asleep at length from sheer exhaustion, and never woke until daybreak. The sky was clouded and our raft was pitching. Gulliver was standing in the middle of the raft, looking at me in evident alarm. I glanced over my shoulder, and the blackness of the horizon told me that a storm was coming, and coming soon.

"I made fast our slender provender, tied the end of a line about my own waist for safety, and waited.

"In a short time the storm struck us in all its tropical fury. The raft pitched and tossed, now high up one end, and now at the other, and sometimes almost engulfed in the waves.

"Gulliver was having a desperate time to keep aboard. His blunt claws slipped on the wet deck of the raft, and he fell and slid about dangerously. The thought flashed across my mind that I might soon be rid of the brute.

121

"As I clung there to the lashings, I saw him slip down to the further end of the raft, his hind quarters actually over the edge. A wave swept over him, but still he clung, panting madly. Then the raft righted itself for a moment, and as he hung there he gave me a look I shall never forget—a look of fear, of pleading, of reproach, and yet of silent courage. And with all my stupidity I read that look. Somehow it told me that I was the master, after all, and he the dog. I could not resist it. Cautiously I raised myself and loosened the square rope I had saved. As the raft tipped the other way Gulliver regained his footing and came sliding toward me.

"Quickly I passed the rope around his body, and as the raft dived again I hung on to the rope with one hand, retaining my own hold with the other. Gulliver's great weight nearly pulled my arm from its socket, but he helped mightily, and during the next moment of equilibrium I took another turn about his body and made the end of the rope fast.

"The storm passed as swiftly as it had come, and though it left us drenched and exhausted, we were both safe.

"That evening Gulliver crept close to me as I talked, and I let him. Loneliness will make a man do strange things.

"On the fifth day, when our provisions were nearly gone, and I had begun to feel the sinking dullness of despair, I sighted a steamer apparently coming directly toward us. Instantly I felt new life in my limbs and

122

around my heart, and while the boat was yet miles away I began to shout and wave my coat.

" 'I believe she's coming, old man!' I cried to Gulliver. 'I believe she's coming!'

"I soon wearied of this foolishness and sat down to wait. Gulliver came close and sat beside me, and for the first time I put my hand on him. He looked up at me and rapped furiously with his tail. I patted his head—a little gingerly, I must confess.

"It was a big, smooth head, and it felt solid and strong. I passed my hand down his neck, his back, his flanks. He seemed to quiver with joy. He leaned his huge body against me. Then he bowed his head and licked my shoe.

"A feeling of intense shame and unworthiness came over me, with the realization of how completely I had misunderstood him. Why should this great, powerful creature lick my shoe? It was incredible.

"Then, somehow, everything changed. Fear and distrust left me, and a feeling of comradeship and understanding took their place. We two had been through so much together. A dog was no longer a frightful beast to me; he was a dog! I cannot think of a nobler word. And Gulliver had licked my shoe! Doubtless it was only the fineness of his perception that had prevented him from licking my hand. I might have resented that. I put my arms suddenly around Gulliver's neck and hugged him. I loved that dog!

"Slowly, slowly, the steamer crawled along, but still

123

kept to her course. When she was about a mile away, however, I saw that she would not pass as close to us as I had hoped; so I began once more my waving and yelling. She came nearer, nearer, but still showed no sign of observing us.

"She was abreast of us, and passing. I was in a frenzy!

"She was so near that I could make out the figure of the captain on the bridge, and other figures on the deck below. It seemed as though they must see us, though I realized how low in the water we stood, and how piti-fully weak and hoarse my voice was. I had been a fool to waste it. Then an idea struck me.

" 'Speak!' I cried to Gulliver, who stood watching be-side me. 'Speak, old man!'

"Gulliver needed no second bidding. A roar like that of all the bulls of Bashan rolled out over the blue Pacific. Again and again Gulliver gave voice, deep, full, power-ful. His great sides heaved with the mighty effort, his red, cavernous mouth open, and his head raised high.

" 'Good, old man!' I cried. 'Good!' And again that mag-nificent voice boomed forth.

"Then something happened on board the steamer. The figures came to the side. I waved my coat and danced. Then they saw us.

"I was pretty well done up when they took us aboard, and I slept for twenty-four hours straight. When I awoke there sat Gulliver by my bunk, and when I turned to look at him he lifted a great paw and put it on my arm."

124

Enderby ceased, and there was silence in the room save for the light snoring of Nubbins.

"You took him home with you, I suppose?" I asked.

Enderby nodded.

"And you have him still?" I certainly wanted to have a look at that dog.

But he did not answer. I saw an expression of great sadness come into his eyes as he gazed out of the window, and I knew that Jacob Enderby had finished his story.

Gun Shy

by EDWARD FENTON

Every day the mornings in the country turned chillier. The sycamore outside the kitchen window was soon bright yellow, and the trees all down the lane made a high arch of burning colors. When Joel stepped out of the house his breathing made little cold clouds of white vapor in front of his face.

This morning was early. Muggsy hadn't even finished his cereal yet. The Duchess ran ahead of him sniffing the air excitedly. With a sudden bound she dashed off into the meadow. Joel watched her weaving through the tall, dry grass, her nose to the ground one moment and the next minute springing up like a jackrabbit, her black ears flying.

Then, suddenly, there was a rustling noise and a mass of feathers rose from the clump of grass ahead over their heads. It glistened across the autumn landscape. Then it was winging out of sight.

This story is from US AND THE DUCHESS, by Edward Fenton

126

The Duchess, now standing stiff in the middle of the field like a dog painted on a calendar picture, was looking after it too. When the bird could no longer be seen, she galumphed back to Joel's side.

Henry came toward them from the barn. Joel noticed at once that he had on his old leather hunting jacket, with the celluloid window on the back of it for his hunting license. Pushed back on his head was a red cap with a visor.

"Hi, Henry," Joel said. "Are you going out today?"

"It's the first day of huntin'," Henry asserted. "Ain't missed it in years. Don't reckon I'll miss it today. Got my license, got my gun all oiled back there in th' barn. Ought to be a good day."

"There are lots of birds around this year," Joel said. "The Duchess just flushed one a minute ago. It was a beauty! It went over that way." He pointed toward the Rocky Pasture.

Henry nodded. "I seen it," he said. "As a matter of fact," he went on, "I was thinkin' of takin' the Duchess along. Ain't never tried her out in the field as yet. Might's well see if she's any good or not."

"I'll bet she'll be better than any other dog you ever took hunting," Joel said stoutly. "Won't you, Duch?"

The Duchess, however, was much too busy pursuing a flea near the base of her tail to do anything in reply to Joel's question.

127

The porch door slammed just then.

"Well, here's ol' Muggsy, the great trapper!" Henry called out, swinging him up on his shoulder. Anthony had on a scarlet hunter's cap like Henry's. He looked very proud of it.

"You bet!" Muggsy began. "I'm the best hunter for miles," he announced with no attempt at modesty. "I can catch lions, 'n' bears, 'n', well, anything, 'cause I'm——"

"Oh, come on," Joel said impatiently. "I've got to get you to school. The bus'll be here soon."

They started down the lane together. Joel called back over his shoulder, "Have a good day, Henry. You and the Duchess!"

"Sure," Henry called back. "We'll make out fine together. So long!"

Johnny Nesbitt was in the bus when Joel and Muggsy clambered in. They all sat together, looking out the window. From time to time they could see men, sometimes singly, sometimes in groups, walking along the road. All of them carried guns and had their hunting licenses pinned to their jackets where everyone could see them, and they all wore bright red caps so that other hunters would not mistake them for game as they moved through the woods. Most of them had dogs following along after them.

"Rusty's a good hunter," Johnny Nesbitt said. "He can smell a rabbit a mile away."

"Henry's taking the Duchess out with him," Joel told him in reply. "She's a real hunting dog. I'll bet when I

128

get home Henry'll have so many pheasants he won't hardly be able to carry them all!"

That day school seemed to drag on without end. All through the classes Joel's attention wandered off from his books or the blackboard to the windows. The trees outside blazed against the clear November sky. From time to time he could hear in the distance the sharp crack, crack of a rifle or the high, excited barking of a dog. All his thoughts were with Henry and the Duchess.

The Duchess, so far, had not done anything to demonstrate her true caliber. She hadn't rescued anyone yet, or had a chance to prove herself a heroine. But this time, he knew, she would show her true colors!

The school bus going home seemed to take all afternoon. Why did the driver always have to stop forever, and why did it always take the other kids such a long time to get off? At last it came to a halt with a squeaking of brakes beside the blue letter box marked "Evans."

Joel looked for the Duchess. Usually she knew when it was time for the bus to return, and she sat in the middle of the lane waiting for him. But she wasn't there now. "She's probably still out with Henry," Joel thought, although it did seem odd that Henry would be out hunting all day, and it was now nearly milking time.

He ran up the lane to the house. Muggsy had to puff like a locomotive to keep up with him.

No, the Duchess wasn't anywhere around. And there was Henry, going out to the barn.

129

"Henry, Henry!" Joel cried. "Where is she?"

Henry set down the pails he was carrying.

"Dunno, Joey," he replied slowly.

"Well, didn't you go out hunting and all?"

Henry nodded. "Sure we went out," he said. "She was fine too. Got a good nose on her. In fact she was all right until I raised my gun and fired."

Joel was breathless. "And then what happened?"

"First thing I know there wasn't no Duchess there. She ran off faster'n I could see her go. Looked all over for her. Looked for hours, but I never did find her. Had to come back 'count of it being milking time." Henry put his big hand on Joel's shoulder. "I'm sorry, kid," he said. "I wouldn't have taken her if I'd of known. She's what they call *gun*-shy. She's scared of shootin'."

"But—but where's she now? We've got to find her!" Joel blinked hard.

"No way of tellin'," Henry said, shaking his head. "She's probably hidin' somewheres right now. She won't come back for a while. The woods are full of gunfire."

Supper was dismal. Joel could hardly swallow, and after every few choking mouthfuls he ran out to the porch to whistle. "She might be out there now," he explained.

Mama looked up at the ceiling. "Boys and dogs!" she sighed. "They're the bane of my life!"

But when Joel came back she looked up hopefully. When he shook his head she sighed again, only it was a different kind of sigh.

 130

Muggsy suddenly announced: "Hey, Joey, I got a idea!"

"Can't you *ever* leave me alone, ever?" Joel demanded. "I'm thinking."

"Well, I been thinking too," Muggsy persisted. "I been thinking about how I found her. I betcha you ain't looked under the bridge!"

Joel looked up in amazement. "I never thought of that!" he exclaimed. The next moment he had dashed out of the dining room.

"Put on your jacket!" Mama called, but the front door had already slammed behind him. "Oh, no, you don't, Anthony!" she said firmly as Muggsy began to squirm off his chair. "You're staying right here."

Joel ran headlong into Henry, who had been out in the barn. "I'm goin'—down to—the bridge," he panted. "To see—if—she's there."

Henry went along with him. They whistled for her at every other step, but there was no Duchess to come dashing up to them in response. They went down the lane together. Joel clenched his fists until his finger-nails dug into his palms.

But under the bridge there was nothing: just the creek trickling in the dark and the stones shining with wetness when the flashlight went on. Joel had never felt so miserable. "Perhaps she got shot, Henry."

"Dunno," Henry said. He shrugged his shoulders and switched off his flashlight. "Come on, kid, better get back.

131

It's cold out here without your sweater. Your ma won't like it. And it won't bring Her Highness back, just standing here and shivering."

They climbed up to the road again and began trudging back to the house.

Suddenly Joel stopped. "Listen!" he whispered.

They stopped. There was a faint pattering sound. It grew louder as they waited.

"Sure it's her!" Joel cried.

And it was indeed the Duchess. She came toward them at a tired trot. Joel ran forward and put his arms around her. He could feel the burs sticking to her coat. She was trembling.

Joel looked up at Henry. "Henry, remember when we first found her? Do you think she might have run off that time the same way? I mean——"

Henry shook his head. "Dunno," he said. "Cain't never tell. Could be."

"But—but that means she's no good for hunting, doesn't it?" Joel thought of Johnny Nesbitt's Rusty, and of how he himself had boasted of the Duchess. He swallowed hard. "But I don't care, Henry," he said, running his hands through the shivering dog's coat. "She needs us more than ever now, and there are worse things than being afraid of guns, aren't there, Henry? Aren't there?"

"Sure," Henry said thoughtfully, "sure. Lots worse things."

Joel stroked the Duchess. "See, Duch," he told her,

 132

"it's all right now. You're home again." He felt as though something inside him was choking him. But he was happy that he had found her again.

"Come on, Henry," he said. "Let's run back. It's cold out tonight."

One Saturday afternoon Joel Evans and Johnny Nesbitt lay spread out, faces downward, upon a nest of dry leaves. Noisily they munched at a couple of frostbitten apples from the basketful which they had gathered for Johnny's mother. Juice dribbled icily down Joel's chin. "I like 'em best this way," he announced indistinctly.

In the deep grass, not far away, waited their fourlegged shadows: Johnny's airedale Rusty and the Duchess. Both were panting gently. From time to time one of them stirred, making a dry rattling sound among the crisp leaves.

It was almost evening. The air was getting keen. The faces of the boys were raw from the wind. Their eyes shone. Their ears and the tips of their noses tingled.

It had been an exhausting Saturday, and all four of them were tired. Not that they had, any of them, much to show for it. Sure enough, there was the basket of apples for Mrs. Nesbitt. It had been fun climbing the trees and shaking them down, while the dogs barked furiously at the rain of fruit which thudded and plummeted to the hard ground. And there was a pleasant aching in their arms and legs from all the fields they had scrambled

133

across, the brooks they had jumped over (one of Joel's socks was wet from the time he had missed), the gullies and ravines they had explored all through the sharp, sun-shot day.

For the dogs there were the thousands of exciting smells to remember and the miles of countless mysterious tracks which they had pursued, yipping frantically. Knowingly, they rolled their brown eyes at their masters.

Joel turned his head and stared at the darkening sky. "Gosh, Johnny, it's getting late. I'd better think of making tracks before Mama sends out a posse." He stretched lazily, then rolled back on the ground, folding his arms behind his head.

"My mother'll be worrying too," Johnny said. "It's funny; she knows I'm all right. Nothing ever happens to me. But she always worries just the same. She ought to be used to me by now!"

"I know," Joel agreed. "They ought to relax more, but they never do. I guess that's the way they are. You just can't change them."

They both lay there, wondering why mothers worried the way they did. But neither of them stirred an inch to get up and start home.

The Duchess pulled herself out of her bed of leaves, stretched luxuriously, yawned with a great creaking of her jaws, and looked at Rusty to see what he was doing. He was engrossed in the serious business of licking a forepaw.

134

The Duchess turned her back to him and moseyed over to where Joel lay.

Joel scratched her chin. "How's the girl?" he demanded. "How's Her Highness?" In reply, she licked his face until he had to raise himself, laughing, to a sitting position.

Johnny got up then, too. They both sat among the dead leaves of the past summer and wondered where the day had gone to.

"It's been one super day," Joel said. He looked around him, at the dark trees against the setting sun. Below them —it seemed far, far below, although he knew it was only a few minutes' run—snuggled the Nesbitt farmhouse. The lights were already on. The windows glowed yellow and smoke twisted from the chimney. He picked another apple out of the basket and bit into it.

It was a good apple, firm and juicy. Joel looked at Johnny and winked; Johnny winked back. Then Joel looked at the Duchess. She had her head slightly to one side and her brown eyes were regarding him with all the trust and faith in the world. Suddenly Joel felt an overwhelming contentment sweep over him. It didn't matter about her being gun-shy, about anything. It was just perfect sitting there with her and Johnny as the sun was setting, and eating an apple. It was a moment he wanted to make last forever. "Stop, clock," he wanted to shout. "Just leave your hands where they are for a while."

135

Finally he said, and it seemed to him as though his voice came out strangely quiet and small, "I don't know any other place I'd rather be than right here now. Do you, Johnny?"

"Sure," Johnny said. "Lots of places. Top of the Empire State Building in New York. Or flying over Shangri-la in my own B-29. The '*Johnny N*' I'd call it, and I'd have the name painted right on her, big. That's the life!" Johnny's eyes began to glisten with excitement.

"Or I'd like to be in a foxhole at the front with a little old machine gun cradled in my arms. Rattatatattat! I'd show that enemy a thing or two or three. They could shoot and shoot at me all they liked. They'd only miss. I wouldn't even hear it! Then me and Rusty—he'd be my Specially Trained Combat Dog—we'd jump out of that foxhole and give them the rush. Just the two of us; we'd take them all prisoners." Johnny clicked his tongue. "That's where I'd like to be. Not stuck out here where it's the same thing all the time, no excitement.

"And what's more," he added, in a confidential tone, "as soon as I'm old enough to do it, I'm gonna join up. And Rusty's coming right with me. I'll bet they could use a smart dog like him in the Army. He's so tough I bet he could easy get into the Marines!"

Joel was scratching the Duchess slowly behind the ear. He didn't say anything.

"Hey, Joey," Johnny went on—he grew more and more

136

excited as the idea became clearer—"you could come too. How'd you like that? And take the Duchess!" He looked eagerly at Joel. "What do you think of that?"

The look on Joel's face stopped Johnny short. "Oh, gee, Joey, I forgot about the Duchess. I mean, about her bein'—"

Joel jumped to his feet. "Oh, that's all right, Johnny. We sort of had other plans anyway." He tried to sound offhand. "And anyway, we have to start trekking home now. I guess it's pretty late."

"Sure," Johnny said. "Sure. And my mother will give it to me good if I don't get those apples home to her!"

Johnny and Rusty walked Joel and the Duchess as far as the glen in silence.

"So long, Johnny," Joel called as he turned off. "See you Monday."

"So long," Johnny called back.

The faint trail across the glen was the shortest way home and Joel wanted to get there before dark. The sun was pretty low already.

The Duchess was off after some scent in a clump of bushes. Her nose was to the ground and her white plume of a tail cut through the twilight. Joel whistled to her. She paid no attention to his call.

Joel's mellow mood of happiness and contentment had completely vanished. In its place he was seized by an unreasoning rage.

137

He whistled again. She was utterly useless, he thought furiously. A gun-shy bird dog. Everybody laughed at her. And now she wouldn't even obey him when he whistled!

"Come here, you!" he shouted harshly.

She bolted out of the bushes and came toward him. Through the growing twilight he could see how uncertain and surprised she was. Already he felt a faint twinge of shame for having spoken to her as he had. But the senseless anger still boiled inside him.

"You come straight off, the next time I call you," he said gruffly.

Then he struck off across the glen toward home. He stopped at one place long enough to cut a maple switch. As he went on, he slashed viciously now and again at the dark trunks of the trees he passed. The Duchess followed faithfully at his heel. He could hear her pattering evenly behind him but he did not turn his head once or stop to speak to her.

By the time Joel reached home, darkness had already fallen. All the lights of the house were on. From the outside, everything had a warm and friendly look.

"We'll catch it for being late," Joel muttered to the Duchess. Resignedly, he made his way to the back door.

Alma was flying about in the kitchen like a demented banshee. She paused long enough to glance up when Joel came in. "Oh, there you are!" she exclaimed. To Joel's

138

surprise, her voice wasn't at all scolding. "Hurry on upstairs and put on your good pants and a clean shirt," she
said. "Dinner'll be on soon. You don't want to be late
for it."

"I thought I was late already," he said. Then he noticed that she was wearing her best apron, the one with
the white ruffles starched as stiff as cardboard.

"Zowie!" he cried. "What's up? Lord Mayor invite
himself for dinner?"

"Never you mind," Alma replied. She pushed him to
the door and waved him up the staircase. "I've got work
to do. You'll find out what's up soon enough when you
come down again."

Joel scratched his head and started up the stairs. Half-
way up he had a sudden idea. "It's not Ellen home for
the weekend, is it, Alma?" he called hopefully down the
stairwell.

"It is not," Alma called back. "And don't forget to
comb your hair and take that scrubbing brush to your
nails," she added. "I'll go tell your ma you'll be right
down."

While Joel changed his clothes and washed, the Duchess pattered after him from his bedroom to the bathroom
and back again. He could hear, faintly, voices floating up
from the living room. He wondered what was happening.
At first he decided that Mr. and Mrs. Grant had come to
dinner. But then Alma wouldn't have put on her best

139

apron just for them. Maybe it was an important business friend of Papa's.

"Dr. Watson, I am compelled to admit that I am completely baffled this time," Joel said, frowning into the mirror. Then, after a brief tussle between his cowlick and his brush (the cowlick won), he switched off the light and went downstairs to the living room.

He saw Mama first. She had on a long dress and her heavy silver Indian bracelets. She was saying something which he couldn't hear and she smiled as she spoke. She looked different from the way she did every day. Joel had forgotten how young and pretty his mother could look. Papa stood behind her, beaming.

Mama turned her head and saw Joel. "And here's Joey!" she announced. Laughing gaily, she pulled him into the room.

Then, suddenly, Joel realized why Alma was wearing her number-one starched apron and why Mama had on her long dress and such a radiant look and why even Papa was smiling openly. Leaning against the mantelpiece, his back to the fire, stood a tall, grinning young man in the khaki uniform of a lieutenant.

"Uncle Seymour!"

The grin widened. "Hi, Joey!"

It was a long time since Joel had seen his uncle. That had been before Uncle Seymour had gone overseas. Joel ran forward. He wanted to rush up and throw his arms around his uncle. But when he came up to him, Joel suddenly stiffened self-consciously and held out his hand instead.

Gravely they shook hands.

Muggsy, who had been quiet and awed, suddenly came to life. "Look, Joey," he cried. "He's got a gold bar on his shoulder. That means he's an officer now. And lookit all the medals he won." Muggsy stood on his tiptoes, running his forefinger across the row of service ribbons pinned to his uncle's tunic. "This one's for Good Conduck. This one's for——"

"Anthony!" Mama said. "Must you always handle everything you see?"

"I was only showing Joey!"

"Well, Joel can see for himself."

Joel could indeed see for himself. His uncle seemed to be taller, somehow, than last time. His face had a lean, almost tired look about it. Joel's eyes took in every detail of the uniform, with its knife-sharp creases, the gold insignia, and the row of ribbons. On one of the ribbons there were little stars. They stood for battles, Joel knew.

His uncle was smiling. "Don't pay any mind to those ribbons, Joey," he said. "They're only my brag rags. Fruit salad, we call 'em."

Joel smiled back at him. "Gosh, Uncle Seymour—I mean Lieutenant!—it's good to see you. When did you get back?"

"I hopped a plane over there only three days ago, and here I am!"

141

Papa began to whistle "Off we go into the wild blue yonder." He caught Uncle Seymour's eye and they both began to laugh.

"Oh, Charlie!" Mama wailed. "There you go. I don't see where that's so funny. Honestly, when you two get together, you carry on just like a couple of overgrown schoolboys."

That only made them laugh harder. "Listen to Grandma!" Uncle Seymour roared. "Relax, Ellie. You look too pretty tonight to pull that stern, serious stuff on us!"

Then Mama gave him a little push. "You!" she said, and she began to laugh too. She didn't look much older than Ellen right then! Joel and Muggsy looked on, grinning. The whole room seemed to be full of happiness and warmth and laughter.

There were candles on the dinner table. Whenever Alma came in, Uncle Seymour teased her and made her blush, but Joel decided that she really liked it, especially when he got up and made a speech.

He said in his speech that he wanted to be on record as being duly, properly, and thoroughly appreciative. Alma had outdone herself as an exponent of the culinary art and Uncle Seymour knew personally of several regiments that would have given their collective eyeteeth to have had her with them overseas.

"Aw, go on with all your talk!" said Alma. She got as red in the face as a poppy, but she loved every word of it.

142

They remained at table a long time. Papa asked Uncle Seymour a great many serious questions, and Joel didn't dare interrupt. Muggsy tried to several times, but Papa's most sarcastic tone of voice managed to squelch him.

Finally Mama rose, which was the signal for them to go back to the living room. The Duchess was already there, comfortably ensconced on the rug in front of the snapping fire.

"Well, look who's here!" Uncle Seymour said. He turned to Mr. Evans. "Charlie, I thought you hated dogs. Where'd you ever pick this one up?"

"I still abominate the noisome yapping creatures," Mr. Evans answered. "This particularly ill-favored specimen happens to be a waif. It is only suffered on the premises because for some mysterious reason my children seem to have become hysterically attached to it."

"She's a beauty," Uncle Seymour said. He knelt and stroked her warm hair. She thumped her tail lazily against the floor.

"I found her," Muggsy said. "She was under the bridge and I found her!" Between them, the Evanses poured out the story of how the Duchess came to be with them.

"So!" Uncle Seymour said. He turned to Mr. Evans. "And is she a good hunter, Charlie?" he asked.

Joel swallowed hard. What would Uncle Seymour think if he found out the truth about her? It didn't matter with most people. But Uncle Seymour was different. Besides, he was a soldier.

143

Tensely, Joel watched his father and waited to hear what he would say.

Mr. Evans cleared his throat.

"Charlie!" Mama said warningly.

Joel didn't dare to swallow again.

"Hm," Papa said. "Well, as a matter of fact—hm—to tell the precise truth—I haven't had her out in the field myself, so-hm—I couldn't exactly testify."

Joel shot his father a grateful glance.

But they had reckoned without Muggsy. The youngest Evans had never been at a loss for words. This time was no exception.

"But Henry took her out, Uncle Seymour. And do you know what? She ran away. She's gun-shy!" He turned triumphantly to his brother. "Isn't she, Joel?"

It was Mama who broke the ensuing silence.

"Up to bed with you," she said. "This Very Minute," she added. It was her firmest tone of voice. From past experience, Muggsy knew that it was the one Mama used when she Meant Every Word She Said.

With a carefully assumed "I-don't-care" look on his face, Muggsy got up from the footstool where he had been sitting and started for the stairs. Uncle Seymour's voice, booming across the room, stopped him in his tracks.

"What I want to know is, what's so awful about being gun-shy?"

Muggsy turned and looked around at his uncle. His eyes were wary with suspicion.

 144

"I'm gun-shy myself," said Uncle Seymour. Joel gaped incredulously at the bright ribbons awarded for valor which were pinned to his uncle's chest.

"Yes, Joey," his uncle said. "You can look at those all you like. But in spite of them I'm still gun-shy. Most of us were, although we didn't always admit it. It scared the dickens out of us when those big guns used to go off. Only there we were, and there was nothing we could do about it, so we had to be heroes."

"But—but—" Joel stammered.

"Sure, after a while we got used to it," his uncle said more quietly. "But if I'd have been able to bolt the first time, I'd have gone like a lubricated lightning streak. And practically all the other men with me would have, too."

Joel and Anthony stared at him.

Their uncle's voice lowered to a confidential whisper. "And you know, even though it's all over, I still dream about those guns sometimes." He thoughtfully shook his head. "And take it from me, chum, those are pretty bad dreams to have."

Mama broke in. "Seymour," she said, "I do think it's time they went to bed. Both of them, in fact. It's been a big night, and there's all tomorrow ahead of us."

After Joel and Muggsy had said good night and started up the stairs, the Duchess got up and cocked her head after them. Then, wagging her tail, she made her way up to bed behind Joel.

Long after Muggsy had fallen asleep Joel lay awake in

145

the dark, staring at the ceiling. He was trying to make up his mind about what Uncle Seymour had said.

It was hard to figure out exactly. There was something funny somewhere.

Imagine admitting that you were afraid of guns and battle and all that kind of thing! Especially when you were a soldier! He would never have dreamed of admitting to Johnny Nesbitt that he had often wondered just how exciting being a real soldier would be. But Joel had always had his private doubts.

And now it was Uncle Seymour who had confirmed them! And he was no coward. He'd been through plenty, and he knew what it was like if anyone did, Joel guessed. Joel lay staring at the dark ceiling, trying to imagine what Uncle Seymour had gone through those nights when he lay in his foxhole with the guns going off all around him. The quiet room became alive with imaginary tracer bullets spitting from planes and the whine of artillery shells.

Joel's arm stole around the Duchess. She was breathing quietly in her sleep. Somehow everything had changed around. It was as though a weight which had been pressing against his chest had been miraculously lifted. He wasn't going to be ashamed of her any more for something she couldn't help.

"Well, Duch," he whispered, "I guess there are lots worse things than being gun-shy." He was sure of that now.

Bat

by STEPHEN MEADER

Labor Day was past, and with it the week of pageantry that wound up the vacation season. Pio Carozzi and Mike Ciliano came out of a small Italian restaurant back by the railroad and sauntered over to their parked sedan. Carozzi plied a toothpick and eyed the golden September day without enthusiasm. "Things are slowin' up, down here," he remarked, as his companion started the car.

"Yeah. Well, we ain't gotta stay much longer," Ciliano grunted. "What'll we do now? Go over an' have a look at the walk?"

"Okay with me. Not much else goin' on."

They left the sedan in North Carolina Avenue and climbed the ramp to the boardwalk. A few steps south brought them to a pavilion with benches, built over the beach. They lighted cigarettes and sat down there to watch the thinning crowds go past.

"I'm gettin' fed up wid this place," said Ciliano. "How 'bout haulin' back to Philly tonight?"

This story is from BAT, by Stephen Meader

147

"Maybe," Carozzi nodded. "Hm—looka the dog."

"Dog nothin'!" his companion grinned. "Get an eyeful o' the dame!"

"Yeah, she's okay," murmured Carozzi. "But the dog—ever see a mutt like that?"

"What about him, outside o' bein' white, an' all slicked up?"

"That's a dog worth a lotta dough, I shouldn't wonder. Like they win prizes with in the dog-shows. I was just thinkin'—you know old man Lucca?"

Ciliano swung slowly around on the bench and looked at him with increasing interest. "Yeah," he said softly. "Yeah, I getcha. He's nuts about 'em—that's right. Maybe you think we could do a job, huh?"

"It don't hurt to look things over, anyway. How 'bout takin' a little walk?"

They rose, stretched, and tossed away their cigarettes. When the slim blond girl and her dog were fifty yards up the boardwalk they sauntered casually in the same direction. A block farther on they saw her stop to speak to another girl, evidently an acquaintance. The voices sounded happy and excited.

"Come on," muttered Carozzi, and he led the way to the railing a dozen feet from the chattering pair. There the two young men leaned, looking down on the beach and listening.

"Yes, isn't he lovely?" the yellow-haired girl was saying.

148

"I'd forgotten you hadn't seen him before, Annabelle. Bat—speak to the lady. Hasn't he nice manners?"

The other girl was duly enthusiastic. "He's simply gorgeous, June!" she exclaimed. "I suppose you've shown him, haven't you?"

"Shown him! Why, my dear, hadn't you heard? He took best of breed in the Westminster. A champion in his puppy year!"

She lowered her voice but the listening men could catch a few of the words. " . . . offered a perfectly tremendous price . . . turned him down . . . oh, yes—Father's just as crazy about Bat as I am!"

Ciliano's elbow touched Carozzi's on the rail. "Got a cigarette?" he asked huskily. "Sounds good, huh?"

When the girls separated, a moment later, the one with the dog turned southward again. She walked with a brisk, athletic swing, and the men trailing her had to quicken their pace to keep her in sight. It seemed to be a long distance to her home. Past the immense façade to the Auditorium and on, block after block. It was farther down the boards than either of the men had ever walked before.

"Where's she goin'?" Mike complained. "Ain't she got a car, or why all this hikin'?"

"Shut up," said Pio. "It's all jake. This is where the real class stays, down here. See them swell joints, with grass around 'em? We're gettin' near Ventnor."

149

At last the girl and the dog turned to the right, and the pair who had been following half a block behind reached the street corner in time to see them going up the gravel drive of an imposing house.

"Don't stop to rubber, sap," warned Carozzi out of the side of his mouth. "Keep walkin'. We got the lay-out now. Nex' time we come in the car."

His pal nodded. "Some dump, huh? Say—maybe that pup IS worth big dough!"

They went on a few blocks before turning back. Knowing where the dog lived was one thing. Putting their plan into action was something else again. "It don't look so hot," Carozzi admitted. "Not if they lead him around all the time with that strap. Prob'ly they keep him in the house nights, too."

"Yeah? Lookit, Pio—there on the beach!"

Trotting along the wet sand at the edge of the tide, Carozzi saw the white dog—all alone.

"Wanna try it right now?" Ciliano whispered.

"Don't be crazy. There's people on the beach could see us. Wait till we got the car handy."

They strolled on up the walk, stealing an occasional glance behind them at the preoccupied bull terrier. Then Carozzi urged his companion to a quicker pace. "We'll go back an' pack up our stuff," he said. "I wanna try it tonight."

An hour later they stowed their luggage in the car and drove to the restaurant where they had been getting their

150

meals. "Wait here a minute," Pio ordered. "I been wonderin' if we can handle him. He looks like he'd take a piece out of a guy he didn't like. Maybe Jakey'll know what a pup goes for."

He returned soon with a small brown paper parcel. "Liver," he explained. "All dogs an' cats is nuts about it, Jakey says."

It was six-thirty when they rolled quietly into Ventnor. Mike drove down a side street toward the boardwalk, turned the car and parked by the curb. They were partly screened from the house by shrubbery. A clink of crockery and a chatter of voices came indistinctly from the servants' wing.

Pio lighted a cigarette. "Wait here," he said. "I'll take a look an' see if he's still down on the beach."

He had the door half open when Mike seized his arm. "Hold it!" he whispered. "The pup's comin' now. I spotted him in the rear-view mirror."

Sure enough, Pio heard a brisk patter of feet on the pavement and turned to see the white dog trotting toward them. He reached behind him for the parcel of liver and unwrapped it hastily. When the terrier was almost abreast of them he cleared his throat and spoke, huskily. "Here y'are, boy—here, Bat! Get a smell o' this. Lookit—liver!"

He glanced warily up and down the empty street and held out the bit of meat toward the dog.

Bat was occupied with his own affairs. The coaxing

151

voice meant nothing to him, even when it spoke his name. He would have gone on without paying further attention to the strangers if that tantalizing scent had not suddenly wafted past his nose. He was hungry, and the smell of liver was more than he could resist. It was only a second he hesitated. Then his tail began to wag and he trotted over to the sedan.

The man who had spoken to him was standing by the open rear door now. As Bat came close he climbed inside and snapped his fingers, holding up the scrap of meat invitingly. Bat jumped in and the door closed after him.

"Let's go!" said the man, in a nervous whisper.

There was only a bite of liver, Bat found. He bolted it in one swallow and sniffed at empty brown paper for more. Meanwhile the man in the rear seat had reached forward and taken a firm grip on his collar.

"Cut over a couple o' streets, Mike, an' get rollin'," he was saying. "I'll keep him down out o' sight."

Bat had no particular liking for these two swarthy young men with the heavy, nose-filling scents. One of them smelled of garlic and the other of hair-oil. However, most humans were unsatisfactory that way. Only one smell really mattered, and that was the dainty fragrance of his golden-haired owner. He thought of her now and wriggled on the floor of the car.

"Sit still, you!" muttered Carozzi, and Bat sat quiet.

The car had been zigzagging through Atlantic City's back streets. Now it was running more smoothly, picking up speed on a straight road. After a while Pio turned his head cautiously and looked behind them. The highway was empty. "Okay, pup," he said. "You can come up here now."

The dog jumped up on the seat and looked eagerly out at the flat Jersey landscape. Mike Ciliano, at the wheel, spoke sullenly. "Gettin' brave, huh? Somebody'll see him."

"There ain't nobody to see him. Besides, he didn't like it down there. He acted like he was gettin' ready to make trouble."

Bat had always liked to ride in cars. This one was a poor substitute for the open roadster but at least it was fun to watch the country shoot past. Behind them now he saw that unbelievable skyline of fairy towers, gold and rose in the sunset, rising mirage-like between desolate marsh and empty sea.

The wide road bore to the right, then to the left through a huddle of small houses. There were a few people in sight and none who showed any interest in the little sedan. After that, concrete ran straight, with sand and scrub pine thickets and lonesome-looking filling-stations on either side.

Carozzi reached over and unbuckled the bull terrier's collar. "Geez," he murmured. "It's silver, an' heavy, too.

153

Here's the doll's name on it. 'June Faulkner, Devon, Pa.' Hey, Mike, I bet I've seen this dame's picture in the society page."

"Yeah?" growled Ciliano. "Well, you better get rid of it. No cars comin', an' plenty o' woods along here."

Pio rolled down the window and threw the collar as far as he could into the brush. Puzzled, Bat watched it glint in the twilight and fall out of sight among the trees. He knew he had been over this road before. There was something familiar about the long parade of sand and woods, dusty hot-dog stands and advertising signs.

They rode in silence for half an hour. "How's he actin'?" Mike asked at last.

"Swell. He likes it," answered Pio. "Turn on your lights. It's gettin' dark."

As they neared Camden and whirled along the brightly-lit boulevard, Bat was coaxed down off the seat to the floor. "Stay there now, feller," Carozzi told him. "You're pretty easy to see."

The car was moving in a stream of traffic now. There were a couple of stops for lights and finally they crept forward in line while the driver fished in his pocket for bridge-toll. At that moment Bat caught a hostile dog smell through the gasoline fumes. He was up at the window in a bound and saw a chow growling at him from another car three feet away. Before he could growl back, Carozzi's quick hands jerked him down. A bell pinged

154

as Mike paid toll, and they shot ahead up the slope of the bridge. "Think they saw him?" Mike asked huskily.

"Not a chance! But you better lay off steppin' on the gas. There's a bridge-cop in back of us, an' he might get nosey."

Bat was allowed no more sight-seeing, but he felt the car swerve to the left and grind along in traffic after the rumble of the bridge was behind. Down there in the dark on the swaying floor-boards he began to grow uneasy. It was long past his supper time, and his instinct told him they were no longer on the route by which he had first traveled to the shore. He decided he liked the dark young man less than ever.

Pio Carozzi breathed easier when they were in the criss-cross of streets that made up South Philadelphia's Little Italy.

"In the alley, back o' my place," he told his companion. "We gotta dig up another collar for this mutt, 'fore we take him anywhere."

Mike guided the car up one dirty street and down another, peered behind him cautiously and swung into the blackness of a ten-foot gap between two old brick houses. For a few yards they jolted over rough cobbles, then came to a stop.

"You stay down here an' keep him quiet," Pio said. "I gotta take a look around. If everything's okay I'll be back in five minutes."

155

Ciliano lighted a cigarette, crouching low behind the dash so that the flare of the match would not illuminate his face. He stared back at the white shape on the rear seat and shifted nervously when Bat's yawn ended in a steely click of teeth.

The minutes dragged by. Finally a door opened close by and was shut again quietly. Carozzi's head appeared beside the sedan. "It's all jake," he told his friend. "Old Lucca's down at Morelli's. Soon as I get this collar on the pup we'll go down an' give him an eyeful."

He fumbled in the darkness and buckled a piece of leather strap around the dog's neck. Tied to it was a length of stout clothes-line cord. "Okay," he said. "We'll leave the car here. Come on, Bat. You're goin' for a walk."

They emerged into the glare of street-lights. There were a few youngsters playing on the sidewalk and windows were open up and down the block. From these came music—a wailing accordion and a tenor voice, and somewhere farther away a crowd harmonizing opera to the accompaniment of a piano. It was with something of a swagger that Pio led the terrier down the street. Mike lagged a few steps behind, watching for blue-coats out of the corner of his eye. He still wondered about that moment at the bridge toll-house.

Morelli's garage was one of the gathering places of local sportdom, as well as headquarters for the truckers of the district. Sometimes a dozen big over-the-road jobs in a

 156

single night would jam the concrete floor. That was because of Tim Eakins. Everybody knew that the stubby little Englishman was the best mechanic on heavy duty engines in town.

In the evenings the garage was the place to find Lucca. He was proud of his fleet of ice cream trucks and liked to be around them while they were being groomed. Sometimes he had one or two of his dogs with him.

It was so tonight. Mike Ciliano sidled in ahead and motioned for Pio to follow him. In a part of the floor unoccupied by trucks there was the usual crowd of loafers and hangers-on. Leaning against the wall was old Lucca himself, a fat, dark Sicilian, diamonds flashing on his pudgy hands. There was a big dog beside him— a rangy, rough-coated airedale.

"Hi, guys," said Carozzi. He grinned and glanced down proudly at the white bull terrier. If he had expected to make a sensation he was disappointed. Lucca finished telling a joke and the others laughed dutifully. Joe Ruffo, ex-pugilist and political henchman of the rich Sicilian, flicked a cigarette butt into a corner and took his time about lighting another.

"What kind of a dog d'yuh call that?" he finally asked, with an intentional sneer in his heavy voice.

"How do you like him, huh?" Pio replied amiably. "He's a real show dog, that one!"

"Bull terrier," remarked Morelli. "That ain't much of a show breed. Them's fightin' dogs."

157

Lucca laughed. "Fight?" he asked. "That white feller? He'd get himself dirty!"

Bat was standing quiet. His slim tail waved slowly, peacefully.

Tim Eakins finished adjusting the front brake of a five-ton freight truck and inched the sleeper out from under the cab. He switched off the trouble-lamp and pushed his blond hair out of his eyes with a none-too-clean wrist. There was a tension in the air. He looked at the white dog and sat still, waiting. Once, in his youth on the Limehouse docks, he had seen such a dog as this in action, and the memory of it tingled pleasantly after many years. "Bli-me!" he whispered to himself. "This oughta be a show!"

The argument he listened to was largely one-sided. Carozzi was trying to turn the discussion away from fighting. "The feller I bought him off said he was worth a grand," he whined. "He was hard up for cash, so I got him cheap."

"How much?" grinned Ruffo.

Carozzi hesitated and looked at his confederate. "Three C's," he said finally.

"Haw, haw!" The laughter was general.

"Why, this dog here"—Lucca indicated the airedale, now growling belligerently—"this baby only stood me a hundred an' fifty. An' fight? He'd eat that pink-eared pup o' yours so quick he'd get a belly-ache!"

158

Pio turned toward the door. "Mike," he muttered, "we better be goin'."

At that moment Lucca unsnapped the leash from the rough-haired dog's collar. "S-s-s-s! Get him, boy!" he said.

There was a breathless snarl, and a black-and-tan streak crossed the open space. Carozzi's legs were knocked from under him—the cord twitched out of his hand. He landed on the concrete and rose dizzy and cursing. The nasty, throaty sound he had been conscious of during his moment on the floor ended abruptly. Everybody was staring toward the corner, where a whirling mass of white and dark resolved itself into the figure of a bull terrier with rigid legs braced, and something limp and furry gripped in his iron jaws. Bat's eyes were blissfully shut. He jerked his powerful neck up, back and down again.

From Lucca came a squawk of fear. "He's killin' him!"

Joe Ruffo tossed away his cigarette and crouched over the dogs. "Naw," he said. "He's killed him."

"Pull 'em apart!" . . . "Get that white devil off him!" . . . "Where's Carozzi? Here—make your dog let go!"

They took hold of Bat's hind legs and pulled. They tried to pry his jaws open. One of the more hysterical bystanders made a grab for Tim Eakins' biggest monkey-wrench but Tim was on his feet by now.

"Drop that!" he said, and jerked the heavy weapon out of his hands. He picked up an empty quart oil tin and ran with it to the gaspump. In a moment he was back.

159

"Look out," he told them mildly, and poured the gasoline over the white dog's nose. Bat sneezed, shivered and released his hold.

"Come 'ere, lad." The little mechanic hooked his fingers into the bull terrier's collar and led him back toward the truck. With clean water he sponged away as much of the gasoline as he could. Finally the choking fumes subsided, and Bat was able to breathe again.

"I 'ated to do it to yer, dearie," Eakins murmured, "but they'd ha' brained yer if I didn't." His hands explored the white hide gently. There were some minor cuts but the blood on the neck was not Bat's.

There was an excited gleam in Lucca's eye as he left the huddle of men around the dead airedale and strode across the floor. Eakins tightened his grip on the white dog's collar. But it was avarice, rather than a desire for revenge, than animated the fat Sicilian.

"Some dog!" he growled, staring down at Bat's erect pink ears. "Some fightin' fool, huh?" He swung away with decision. "Hey, you—Carozzi!" he called.

Bat yawned and licked the blood off his jaws. It was the second fight of his carefully-guarded life. That instinct for combat, bred into his marrow through scores of generations of pit-dogs, had found fulfillment at last.

Gravely he blinked up at the tow-headed young man in greasy clothes, whose fingers scratched so pleasantly behind his ears. Now that the tension of the battle was over he remembered that he was hungry.

 160

The other men were talking in loud voices. Wads of dirty, greenbacked paper changed hands. And now the stout man with the shiny rings on his fingers was coming toward him again.

"This oughta be a quick clean-up," grinned the ice cream maker. "Come on, you mugs. I want to find old Gaetano. He'll put heavy dough on that bow-legged bull-dog he's so proud of."

Tim Eakins watched the crowd go out, taking the white terrier with them. He knew better than to meddle. He'd got along with these people ten years by keeping his mouth shut. But he felt a bitter resentment as he crawled back under the truck. There was a gallant British sportiness about the dog that had made him half home-sick, good American though he was.

Hours later, when he had peeled off his coveralls and was rubbing sand-soap on his hands at the sink, Morelli and Ruffo ran in.

"Where's Joe's car?" snapped the garage-owner. "No—I'll get it. You, Tim, put that dead dog in the back room —under the pile of old tires. The bulls are comin'."

Tim Eakins hid the airedale's body in the back room. As he was returning he heard Ruffo's car go roaring out across the curb. Morelli had gone also. Methodically he sloshed a bucket of water over the blood stains in the corner and went back to scrubbing his hands.

The two men who entered before he finished using the towel were City Hall detectives. The larger one ambled

161

over with a casual greeting. "Seen anything of a white fightin' dog 'round here tonight?" he boomed confidently. Tim shrugged. "I did 'ear some talk o' one," he replied. "Wot's up now?"

"Stole," said the big Irishman. "We got word he might be down this way. A patrolman kept findin' dead dogs in the street. Three of 'em—an' they weren't run over, either. But you know these folks 'round here. They won't talk."

"Gor!" murmured Tim. "Three dead ones, you say? Wot a pup!"

The smaller detective had been wandering restlessly around the garage floor. He stared sourly at the wet place in the corner, then turned to inspect a dirty pair of coveralls hanging on a nail.

"These yours?" he asked the mechanic.

Tim squirmed. There were short, stiff, white hairs clinging to the cloth.

"All right," snapped the detective. "Start talkin'."

" 'Old on, now," the little cockney replied with some dignity. "I didn't say anything about NOT seein' 'im, did I?"

"Okay. Who had him in here?"

"A couple o' young chaps. Strangers to me. I didn't take notice of 'em partickler—only o' the dog. 'E was a bit of all right."

"What did they look like—these two mugs?" The smaller detective had his note-book out.

162

"Both medium 'ight, I'd say. Thin. Dark. One 'ad on a gray suit an' the other a blue serge. Don't remember the kind of 'ats they wore."

"You're a lot o' help," the sleuth grumbled. "Might be any two of a thousand guys. If we pick anybody up we may have to call you to identify 'em."

When they had gone Tim Eakins looked at his silver watch. It was close to midnight. Too late now for him to go and call on his girl, Marie. However, he wouldn't have to be back at work till noon next day so there was no reason to go home for a while. He tied his necktie, put on his hat and locked up the garage. Outside it was a hot night, close and quiet. With his coat over his arm, Tim strolled up the street to the soft-drink place on the corner.

The fat proprietor was drowsing alone at one of the rear tables.

"Hi, Rocco," Tim greeted him. "Where's all the customers?"

Rocco heaved himself out of his chair with a yawn. "They all left here a while ago," he said. "Guess they gone home now."

Tim nodded. "Sars 'parilla," he said, and when the glass and the straws were in front of him, he waited for the Italian to go on. It was evident that Rocco had something on his mind.

After a moment the fat fellow chuckled and rubbed his hands. "By golly!" he said. "I seen something tonight like I never seen before!"

163

Eakins sipped a swallow or two of sarsaparilla. "The dog, you mean?" he asked without too much eagerness.

"Yeah—was you there too?"

"Just the start—at the garage. Wot 'appened after that?"

"Geez!" Rocco breathed. "What a dog! They fought him four times—five times—in two hours. The ol' man—" he looked around hastily and lowered his voice, "—the ol' man cleaned up two grand in bets, they say!"

Tim's eyes widened. "You mean 'e won every time?"

"All but the last time." Rocco picked up a wet rag and wiped off the bar. "The white dog was tired, maybe. What I hear, they give him a police dog—twice as big as him—an' the police dog finished him off. Then they heard the cops was comin' an' everybody scrammed."

Tim swigged down the last of his drink and laid a dime on the counter. "So long, Rocco," he said, and walked back to his little old car, parked in the alley behind the garage. His heart was heavy on that drive home to Camden, across the river. "Dirty dagoes!" he growled once, aloud. Then he remembered that Marie was Italian, too. "Dirty 'umans!" he corrected himself.

The Dog Who
Chose a Prince

by CATHERINE CATE COBLENTZ

This is a true story of Holland, in the days when the Dutch people were struggling for freedom against the Spanish King who ruled them and taxed them heavily against their will.

Long, long ago a small black spaniel howled mournfully through the night, as he shivered outside the high walls guarding the Dutch city of Delft. He was wet and cold and his feet hurt. He had traveled all day. He had swum ditches and canals, crossed fields and followed dusty roads. But always he had gone toward the sweet sound of the Delft bells. Something besides the sound of the bells had drawn him toward the city. Something seemed to tell him that here at last he would find the master he had been seeking.

When morning came, the spaniel howled no longer. He was too tired. But when the crowds of people gath-

This story is from STORY PARADE magazine

165

ered in one place, he slipped in among them. There were peddlers and vagabonds and honest country-folk bringing their vegetables and chickens, and even their little fat pigs to market.

The little dog's eyes wandered from face to face and his ears listened to the voices. But if he saw a face he liked, he did not like the voice. Not a man nor a woman, nor a boy did he see and hear, whom he would choose for his master.

He sighed a little, for it was clear he had not undertaken an easy task. And then he heard the sound of many horses coming down the road.

The horses held their heads proudly, even though they had journeyed a long way. The men wore uniforms of blue and gold. One of them carried a banner of orange with these words written on it: "I shall carry on."

Then the little dog heard a voice which was deep and at the same time gentle and filled with beauty. It was like the sound of the bells which had led the dog through the night.

"The city is gold and silver in the sun," said the voice. "It is a good city and a good land. I shall strive to keep the rights which these cities have gained and give this land the freedom it deserves."

The little dog looked into the face of the speaker. The face was thin and lined, as though the man had suffered much. But his brown eyes had a marvelously kind ex-

166

pression. This man, he decided, should be his master.

Just then some one cried, "See, the drawbridge falls."

The drawbridge had indeed fallen over the moat, and the great door of the city gate was opened. The horses bearing the blue-and-gold-dressed riders dashed over the bridge.

The spaniel leaped quickly from the crowd. He must follow them. He must follow the man whom he had chosen for his master!

But the people who had been waiting for the city gate to open surged forward and made a wall of legs between the spaniel and the horsemen. The spaniel dashed to one side and the other, but he could not get through. Finally he dashed underneath an ox-cart. And in this fashion he entered the city.

There were boats slipping along the canals, and there were many people and much laughter. There was a great market where all the country folk were gathering. And here and there was a horse. But the spaniel found no trace of the crowd of horsemen with the man whom he had chosen in their midst.

Up one canal and down another, the little dog wandered. Through this narrow street and that he went, sniffing and listening and watching. At last he came to the saddler's house, and the saddler, who was fond of animals, invited the dog to come in. He gave the spaniel a good breakfast. Then he opened the door to a little courtyard, where there was a fountain and pigeons, and said, "Come out and rest in the sun, for I must finish this saddle. It is for an Important Person."

The dog was not the least bit interested in an Important Person. So, with a full stomach he lay down in the sun on the warm bricks of the courtyard and put his nose in his paws. Soon he was fast asleep. He dreamed, and when he awoke, he thought he was still dreaming. For he could hear the voice of the man whom he had chosen for his master.

"It is a fine saddle," said the voice. "Clearly you are a Master Workman, for I have never had a better."

The dog hurled himself at the door, barking sharply. "Let me in," said the bark. "Let me in. This is an important matter! A most important matter!"

But the door to the courtyard remained closed. And when at last it did open, the Important Person had gone. The dog leaped to a little chest beside the window and looked out. Yes, it was the same. His ears, his nose had not deceived him. Now he filled his eyes with the sight of his chosen master.

"The Prince of Orange knows good work," said the saddler.

The dog barked once more. But it was useless. Down the narrow street the man went and turned a corner. The dog started to whine. Then he stifled the whine, for he saw that the saddler had forgotten him. The man threw

168

wide the door and stepped briskly down the street. He must tell his friend, the weaver, how the Prince of Orange had praised the saddle he had made.

But the spaniel did not wait. Even as the saddler opened the door, the dog was out of the saddler's house and headed for the corner where his chosen master had disappeared.

It was easy enough, he found, to trail the Important Person, if he kept his head low and sniffed along the ground. Finally he came to a house under some linden and willow trees. Here the trail ended.

So the spaniel sat down on the white-scrubbed walk and waited. He had learned that if one only waited long enough, doors that were closed would open.

This time it happened as it had before. A man came with a letter in his hand, and the door was opened. The spaniel fairly flew through the air, and he managed to get inside beside the messenger before the door closed. As luck would have it, he dashed straight into the open room where the Prince was sitting before a great table.

"What . . . ?" came the voice.

"Only a dog, sire," said the servant, banging his head as he reached under the table to haul forth the spaniel. Before the Prince had even seen him, the dog found himself outside.

"Be off," said the servant sharply.

But the spaniel did not go far. The moment the door

169

was closed, he crept back and sat down on the white-scrubbed walk once more.

A second time he managed to slip in, and a second time a servant drove him out.

When for a third time the dog succeeded in entering the house, he jumped straight into the lap of his chosen master.

"Let me look at this persistent one," laughed the Prince. The spaniel wiggled with delight at the sound of that laugh, for it was free and deep.

The Prince turned the little dog's head upward, and the kind eyes of the man looked deep into the eyes of the dog. The spaniel tried to put all that he felt in the look which he gave back to the man. He tried to say how he had set forth to choose a master and how he had chosen the Prince from the moment he had seen him. He tried to explain how he had hunted for him all through the city.

Strangely enough, the Prince of Orange understood. For after a silence he asked, "Would you like to remain with me, then?"

The spaniel barked and his tongue darted toward the man's fingers.

"A nuisance, your highness," protested the servant.

"Perhaps . . . perhaps a friend!" The voice had a strange hushed tone in it. And the dog understood that the man needed him as much as he himself needed the man.

 170

Wherever the Prince of Orange went, the spaniel went, too

171

"Will you serve me faithfully?" asked the voice, very softly. And the man added slowly, "It may not be easy."

The dog's bark was sharp and eager. Again the Prince seemed to understand. He turned and said, "The spaniel is mine. His name—well, it must be imposing. Let me think." Then he laughed aloud. "He looks somehow like my favorite Roman general. That general's name was Pompey."

The dog barked. It was a good name.

So that is how a little Dutch dog chose his master. And wherever the Prince of Orange went, the spaniel went, too, even into battle. Pompey proved himself a good companion. For, when the day was over and cares were heavy on the man's shoulder, the spaniel cheered and comforted the Prince. Those who bear the burden of freedom for others are often lonely themselves. So it was with William of Orange.

Now the Spaniards were determined to put an end to the Prince. For, under his leadership, the Dutch were united in their struggle for freedom. But always the Prince escaped the soldiers of Spain. Always he remained to lead his people.

So it went until the year 1668, when the Prince of Orange pitched his tent near the city of Mons. There he rested, with Pompey on guard, and his own men near in tents close by. Meanwhile, in the camp of the Spaniards, an officer named Romero plotted against the life of Prince William. He planned to do by a trick what the

172

Spaniards had not yet been able to do on the field of battle.

Through a traitor, Romero arranged that the men who guarded the Prince of Orange should be drugged. So, while the Prince worked late in his tent, one by one those about him who should have been watching fell asleep.

Meanwhile through the night came the Spanish soldiers with their leader, Romero. Over their armor they wore long white shirts, so that they seemed like a horde of ghosts in the dark. Like so many snowflakes they slipped across the countryside. Their swords flashed and the sleeping soldiers of the Prince were killed.

Nearer and nearer they came to the tent of the Prince. The Spaniards were triumphant. Let them but kill the Prince, and the King of Spain could do thereafter just as he pleased with his Dutch subjects.

But they had not counted on Pompey, who spent each night by his master's bed. Something in the strangeness of the silence, it may be, wakened him. Perhaps he heard a stifled groan or the sound of a sword clinking on a stone.

At any rate, inside the tent of the Prince of Orange, the spaniel Pompey burst into a sudden torrent of barks. At first, the Prince, who had thrown himself upon his camp cot without undressing, did not waken. Perhaps, he too, had partaken of the drugged food. Perhaps he was simply too weary.

Pompey was certain now that evil things were afoot. He caught new, unknown scents. He heard strange voices.

173

He ceased barking and leaped to his master's bed. His pink tongue licked feverishly at his master's face. His paws tugged at the man's shoulders.

The Prince sat up. He shook his head and he, too, heard strange sounds. He called to the guard outside, but no one answered. He heard a thud and then someone was fumbling at the entrance to the tent.

The Prince waited not a second. He jerked up the tent behind him and crawled underneath. Pompey flattened himself and was at his heels. There was a riderless horse, standing uncertainly in the darkness.

The Prince leaped into the saddle, and the spaniel followed. In one arm the Prince cradled the dog, and the horse, as though understanding the precious burden he bore, moved quietly away from the empty tent. Crouching low, the Prince escaped.

"Only a riderless horse," whispered one Spanish soldier to another.

But another Spaniard came angrily from the tent. "This is the tent. And the bed is warm. But there is no one here. The dog is gone, too."

"That dog . . ." swore Romero, tearing his white shirt in his anger.

But freedom was saved, for the Prince of Orange was saved. The spaniel had served the Prince faithfully. And to this day you will see that the statues of the Prince of Orange—whom the Dutch called the Father of his Country—always have a little spaniel at the man's feet.

174

Pot Likker's First Fox Hunt

by ROBB WHITE

The lights on the caboose got dimmer and dimmer and then were gone. Soon they couldn't even hear Mr. Duncan's engine any more.

This was big, dark, open country. They could see a hill with tall pines on it rising against the night sky.

"That's Widow's Hill," Judy said, whispering. "See those lights down there? That's where the men are letting their hounds out."

They climbed a fence and walked through a neglected pasture dotted with clumps of bushes.

Pot Likker had learned to heel and walked just behind and to Jonathan's right. Whenever he started away anywhere, Jonathan would tell him to heel.

A dirt road wound around the bottom of the hill and cars were coming along it, their headlights streaming out across the broom sage as they approached the corner.

This story is from THE HAUNTED HOUND, by Robb White

175

Judy led the way in a wide half circle until, at last, they could see some parked cars and trucks and a lot of horses.

In the headlights hounds wheeled around. There was a lot of noise with the dogs barking and starting make-believe fights, the men yelling and calling to them, and the horses neighing.

"We'll stay downwind from them so none of those old hounds will come over here bothering us," Judy said, stopping behind a high clump of bushes. "You better hold Pot Likker."

Jonathan said indignantly, "I don't have to hold my dog. I just tell him to sit down and he sits down until I tell him to get up. Pot Likker, sit down."

In the dark, so Judy wouldn't see, he gave Pot Likker a little push, and the dog sat down.

"They're about ready," Judy said, peering around the bushes. Then she squatted down beside Pot Likker. "Tell him to listen to me, Jonathan."

Jonathan squatted down, too, so that Pot Likker was between them. "You listen to Judy," he told Pot Likker.

Judy didn't touch the dog for she had already discovered that Pot Likker didn't like anyone but Jonathan to touch him. But she put her face close to his. "Now, listen, Pot Likker," she said. "You run this race right, hear? I don't know how you've been behaving while you were running foxes by yourself, but if you behave wrong now Jonathan will be ashamed of you.

"Run it right, Pot! Don't say a word until you really

176

know you smell a fox. Don't go to hollering just because you feel good, or because you want all the other dogs to know you're there. Keep quiet, Pot, until you smell that fox. Then you tell 'em, Pot Likker! Talk to 'em. Jonathan will be up on the hill listening for you to speak, so roll it out.

"Don't let the other dogs mess you up. Some of those July hounds can outrun you for a little while, but remember, you've got a long way to go and you'll catch up with them."

Jonathan interrupted her. "They're getting on their horses, Judy," he whispered.

"All right now, Pot. Here you go. Just run it right!"

Jonathan held the big, trembling dog for a little while longer as the other hounds started away. All the car lights were off now, and the dark file of horses wound up toward the top of Widow's Hill.

Jonathan turned him loose at last. "Go, Pot Likker!"

The black-and-white body bounded away. They heard a low, anxious, excited whine and then nothing more.

Judy straightened up. "He started off right anyway," she said. "A lot of dogs will start right off yapping."

"I'm shaking all over," Jonathan said.

"So am I. Oh, I hope, I hope, I hope," Judy said, hugging herself.

"Me, too. What can he do wrong, Judy?"

"Everything! He can start barking before he smells anything. He can start running a deer—Oh, gosh, that

177

would be dreadful. He can get a fox trail and run it back-ward. He can get into a dog-fight. He can get jealous of the dog that's hot on it and try to lead the pack off on a false scent. Or he can just quit."

Jonathan stiffened, looking at Judy in the dark. "Pot Likker won't quit," he said.

"I don't think so, either. But some dogs do. They just haven't got any bottom at all and can't run more than an hour or so. But I've seen some dogs who would run a fox all night long. I saw old Mister Blue one time come in at dawn with all four feet bleeding. Uncle Dan was carrying him back to the truck when he smelled another fox. He got out of Uncle Dan's arms and ran that fox un-til eleven o'clock in the morning. He's dead game all the way through."

Jonathan said quietly, "And he's Pot Likker's father. Pot Likker may do all those other things wrong—and I won't care much if he does—but he won't ever quit."

Judy said slowly, "You never can tell, Jonathan. Some dogs just have that kind of courage and some don't."

"Pot Likker's got it."

Judy smiled slowly at him. "I think he has, too, Jonathan." Then she turned and looked up toward the top of the hill. "They're getting settled down," she said.

Jonathan saw the light of a fire flowing up the trunks of the pine trees and flickering against the dark green needles. "What do they want a fire for?" he asked, amazed, because he was sweating.

178

Judy chuckled. "They always build a fire. Habit, I guess. In the winter it keeps 'em warm. In the summer I guess they use it to see each other with."

Jonathan followed her then as she started up the hill. "We won't go too close," she whispered back. "But I want to hear what they say. Especially if Pot Likker gives tongue."

"I do, too."

As they got nearer to the fire they slowed down, tiptoeing so as not to break twigs or anything. At last Judy halted behind a huge old pine, so old its bark was hard and smooth. She stopped Jonathan with her hand.

Cautiously they peeked around the tree. On logs, or just sitting on the ground, the fox hunters ringed the bright fire. Judy nudged Jonathan and whispered, "That old man with the white beard is Senator Hammond. I know a lot of the others, too. The one in that fancy shirt is my Sunday-school teacher."

Jonathan looked at the men and, suddenly, one of them, his back to Jonathan, looked familiar. He nudged Judy. "Isn't that your uncle Dan? The one nodding his head?"

Judy grabbed Jonathan's arm with both hands. "Ohh, ohh," she said, pushing him back behind the tree. "I got to sit down," she whispered, collapsing.

Jonathan sat down beside her.

"What are we going to do?" Judy asked.

"About what?"

179

"Everything. Uncle Dan'll recognize him if Pot Likker opens his mouth."

"You think so?"

"I know so. Some other men make mistakes saying the wrong dog is speaking, but not Uncle Dan. He'll *know* it's Pot Likker."

"Maybe he'll think Pot Likker just ran away and got into this hunt accidentally."

"Not a chance. Uncle Dan knows Pot's your dog. And he'll know that wherever Pot Likker is you're somewhere close around."

"Can we get Pot Likker away now?"

"I don't see how. They're probably a mile from here and we won't even know where until one of them speaks."

Jonathan thought awhile. "Oh, well," he said sadly, "if we can't do anything, there's no use worrying about it."

"Uncle Dan's a sort of understanding man," Judy whispered. "Sometimes."

Jonathan was about to say something when the voice of a dog cut through the night air. It was as though something had grabbed Jonathan's backbone and yanked it stiff.

"Just a puppy yapping," Judy said.

Jonathan let his breath out and sank back against the tree.

Around the fire the talk of the men was dying down, and Jonathan could almost feel them listening.

 180

Then one of the men spoke. The voice was old and cracked and Jonathan guessed that it was the senator. "Should be about to the branch head now," the old voice said. "If they strike on that old four-toed fox in there, it'll be a race, boys!"

Jonathan leaned around the tree and saw all the men nod their heads.

Another man asked someone, "Bill, have you got that Sarko hound of yours in this race?"

The man named Bill answered, "When you hear a real hound voice coming up here, then you'll know whether my dog Sarko's around here or not."

"Oh, oh," Judy whispered. "That's Mr. Tatum. Sarko is a wonderful dog. He really is. And he's got a voice like a man yelling in a barrel—you can hear him across a county."

A man at the fire asked, "How about Ben Brown?"

"He's in there, too. And I've got a Trigg hound in here tonight that can outrun any fox-chasing dog in the state. Got him right out of the trials up in Kentucky. That dog's got a built-in streak of lightning."

"I seriously doubt," the old senator said, "if any dog here tonight can outrace my Dora. I seriously doubt it."

Judy giggled, but none of the men said anything. "Poor old Dora," Judy whispered. "She's all the senator's got, and he just loves her to death. She used to be a fine hound, too. But now all she is is smart. She knows every trick there is in the world."

181

Jonathan felt tight all over and his fingers were tearing apart all the pine needles he could find on the ground. "There're so many dogs down there," he said, his voice scared.

"*Boy!*" Judy said. "And good ones, too. They don't make foxhounds any better than Sarko and Ben Brown. Maybe that Trigg's good, too." She looked at Jonathan. "Pot Likker's really in a race tonight," she declared.

"I—I'm glad," Jonathan whispered. "He'll do all right. He'll do fine. Won't he, Judy?"

"Sure he will, Jonathan. Of course he's awful young and he hasn't run with a pack before. But just think of all the good things he'll learn. It'll be wonderful for him."

Something was happening. Over by the fire there wasn't any more talk at all. Everyone seemed to be waiting for a sound to come up out of the valley. Everything seemed to be making a hollow place of silence just so Jonathan could hear it when it came.

Jonathan began to listen with his whole body as he sat stiff against the tree, his face toward the dark wooded valley. He stopped hearing the crackling of the fire and the lonesome hooting of an owl. The layer of noise made by the summer wind through the pines, the stomping of the horses, the night bugs, and a mocking bird became like a wall around a silence in which he waited, listening.

He could see nothing down in the dark valley. No movement, no running animals. Nothing. Just deep darkness

 182

where the woods were and a lighter darkness on the open fields.

And it was so silent down there. It was hard for him to believe that a whole pack of foxhounds was running in that dark place.

Then, rolling up out of that valley, there came a voice. It was deep and booming, coming from a big, strong chest. It was a voice that wrapped around you and made you want to stand up and yell.

It nailed Jonathan against the tree, his breath trapped in his throat, his muscles frozen. To him there was nothing else but that voice. Judy wasn't there, nor the fire, nor the men. Just that one great, bugling hound's voice.

He waited a long time, knowing in his heart that it was Pot Likker but waiting anyway to be sure. Then, at last, his whisper broken, he asked, "Is it, Judy?"

"Yes," she said.

It was music, and he thought he was going to burst out crying with happiness.

Then, as sudden and terrible as the screech of automobile tires, Jonathan heard the old senator say, "That's my Dora, boys. She always has made music like that."

All Jonathan's muscles started pushing him to his feet in outrage, but Judy caught him by the arm and pulled him down. Anybody could tell that that voice belonged to a young dog, a big, strong, swift-going dog. Not to an old, old dog.

Judy was whispering to him. "Nobody pays any atten-

183

tion to the senator," she said. "He's old and can't hear very well, and he likes to believe that it's always his dog Dora. Nobody minds, Jonathan. Dora's all he's got."

That one steady voice kept on, all by itself, for a long time—so long that Jonathan began to tremble again. "Is he doing something wrong, Judy?" he whispered. "Why don't the other hounds say anything, Judy?"

"I don't know. He might just be way out in front."

"I can't stand it," Jonathan said pitifully. "What'll we do if he's doing something wrong?"

"Nothing. He'll learn all by himself, Jonathan. But if he's wrong, he ought to be wavering a little by now. If it's a deer, or just nothing at all, he ought not to sound so strong and sure of himself."

But the voice kept on, and it was sure of itself and strong.

And then another hound gave tongue.

Judy clutched Jonathan's shoulder. "That's Sarko!" she whispered in his ear. "Sarko wouldn't speak if it wasn't a fox."

And another bugling voice came up.

"Ben Brown!" she whispered.

Then a high, squealing, coarse voice. "Old Dora. She must have cut. Oh, Jonathan, listen to him! *Listen* to Pot Likker."

Now all the hounds were open, wide, and the valleys and hills were full of sound. But still the deep, bugling music of Pot Likker sounded above them all, and you

184

could tell that he was the only one who had the fox scent hot and fresh. That he was the one out in front of the whole pack.

Jonathan heard one of the men say quietly, "Can't place that first mouth, can you?"

"Sounds a little like Jack Tatum's Sarah, but I'm not sure."

"Couldn't be Sarah. She just whelped. But it's a Trombo anyway."

Then another man said, "You know, that voice sounds like Bill Barrett's old dog Blue. I'd swear that that was Mister Blue if I didn't know that old hound had run his last race."

The first man said, a little louder, "Dan, what dog is that? You haven't put old Blue in there, have you?"

Jonathan and Judy stopped breathing as they waited.

Slowly, "Mister Blue's home under the house, Will," Mr. Worth said. "I don't know what dog that is. But I sure would like to."

Jonathan let out his breath. "Do you think he really doesn't know?"

Judy whispered, "He knows all right. He just isn't telling."

The hound voices died one by one as they lost the scent. Then Pot Likker opened again. There wasn't any maybe in the way he said it; he was on it hot and going out of there, and he was telling the rest of the hounds that they could come with him if they wanted to. But he

185

didn't need any of them to tell him that he had that fox scent so strong he could hold his head up and just run him.

Judy pulled at Jonathan's hand. "We've got to go," she said urgently. "Pot Likker'll tree that fox in a minute and the whole crowd will be around with flashlights."

They got up and, for a while, sneaked away down the hill. When they were in the clear, they began to run as hard as they could.

Then, in a field lit by the rising moon, Jonathan saw them. The pack was strung out, going across the field, and Pot Likker was way ahead, his big black-and-white body stretching out and his voice floating back over him and spreading all over the country.

"Call him off," Judy said, panting. "Quick. Here they come."

As Jonathan tried to stop gasping, he saw the horses wheeling down the hill.

It took him a long time to get enough breath to blow the cow horn, but at last he sent the commanding, long, trailing tune down the valley.

Pot Likker slowly stopped giving tongue.

"That's breaking his heart," Judy said, still whispering, although there was no need for it now.

Jonathan blew once more.

Then Pot Likker came, loping along, miserable, his ears flopping, his tail almost dragging the ground.

Jonathan, his voice choked, grabbed his dog and sat down on the ground. "Oh, Pot," he cried, "you did it!

186

You ran it, and you showed them all how to do it. Oh, Pot Likker!"

The hound looked back and shivered. The other dogs were baying treed and flashlights were skittering around.

The mournful crying of a train whistle floated across the field, and Jonathan stood up.

Judy had already started running, and he followed, watching her gold hair bounce with each step she took.

At the tracks they waited as the freight cars slowly clattered by. In the door of the caboose a man was holding a lantern so that they could see the handrail and the steps.

Judy swung herself up, the man catching her and swinging her to the platform. Then Jonathan went up.

Pot Likker ran along beside the caboose, looking up at Jonathan.

"Come on, Pot Likker. Jump," Jonathan called.

It was so easy and graceful. The big body just seemed to rise and float, the paws tucked up, the long tail streaming out, and the ears flopping around.

Pot Likker landed on the platform and sauntered on into the little room just as though the leap was nothing at all.

187

Ne-Nu-Ka

by ROBERT DAVIS

It was a Saturday morning, and Sandy had been tinkering around the boat house, when a water-logged canoe, with only the prow and the gunwale showing above the water line, came drifting down the Abitibi. Intrigued by the idea of treasure trove, and lured by the ambition of being owner as well as captain of a new craft, he had rowed out in his father's flat-bottomed skiff, and towed the derelict to the Company's dock. Upon two barrels he had turned it upside-down to dry, and was taking stock as to how it might be rendered seaworthy, when he suddenly realized that Little Beaver was standing beside him.

In his unobtrusive manner, Little Beaver had become Sandy's shadow. The Factor's son would come whistling from the kitchen, seeing nobody. Silent as a ghost, the Indian would rise from where he had been squatting on his heels unobserved, beside a tree or woodpile. He was so noiseless that Sandy hardly knew when he came, or

This story is from HUDSON BAY EXPRESS, by Robert Davis

188

when he went. He seemed to foresee exactly what Sandy intended doing next. The white boy would need a tool, or a piece of material. Presto, Beaver would have placed it within reach. He might even undertake the work himself.

Four ribs of the canoe must be replaced. It was Beaver who brought a fresh-hewn, straight-grained log of yellow birch, sliced off the slats, whittled them into the correct form, and with a tourniquet of cord bent them to the proper curve in which to dry.

The repairs were about completed. Sandy had daubed shellac around the cracks and was tacking on patches of canvas. After another coat of the quick-drying varnish the salvaged wreck would be ready for a trial voyage.

Suddenly the boy's gaze fastened upon something beyond the river. "Look, Beaver," he called. "Do you see what I see?"

The Indian crouched under Sandy's pointing finger, and grunted. A grey thread of smoke was rising straight into the windless air.

Smoke means fire. A fire means people. But nobody lived where the fire was. It was neither the place nor the season for hunters or fishermen. The boys knew the whereabouts of all the whites and natives of Porcupine and Indian Village. They were no more than a handful and all accounted for. Sandy continued with his tapping and shellacking, but an imp of curiosity fidgeted within his brain.

189

"These patches are dry enough," he said, straightening his back. "Let's give the old tub a bath." And after an interval, during which, with copper wire, he spliced a new handle to a paddle, he added, "Let's see what they're doing. It looks as though the fire is at Calico Spring. But no one has used that tumble-down lean-to since last April."

"Sure," agreed Beaver. "Eat there, yes?"

"Good idea. I'll get Mother to fix up some grub." Sandy put away his tools and started for the kitchen.

The resurrected canoe no longer leaked, but it was warped and awkward to steer. Upstream a couple of hundred yards they beached it on some sand. Peering through the brush, they advanced cautiously toward the spring, guided by the smoke. Most of the leaves had fallen and they could see a good distance ahead.

Framed by the poplar branches, the picture that met their eyes made them blink with astonishment. Half of the roof of the lean-to had blown away or fallen in, but beneath the remaining end reclined a man either old or feeble, or both. And certainly he was exhausted by exposure and lack of food.

His skin was the tint of a half-breed, and stretched tight as a drumhead over his bones. His frame was big, but muscle and flesh had fallen away, leaving hardly more than the skeleton. Strips of flannel, evidently cut from the blanket spread upon his knees, were wound about his feet. And although it was mid-day and only the end of October,

190

his hands almost touched the smudge of twigs and leaves, so obvious were his sufferings from the cold.

Across the fire from the man sat a dog. The boys were familiar with the breeds of work dog that are the trapland's beasts of burden, the Samoyedes of Siberia, the Huskies of Greenland and Labrador, the Malemutes of Alaska, the mongrel strains of the Indians, and with the color combinations of these breeds and their crosses. They knew dogs as boys further south knew the model of bicycles and motor cars. But such an animal as this they had never seen. Whereas the work breeds all have wolf blood in their distant ancestry, this dog, by the boys' best guess, possessed the blood of the white Arctic wolf, but it had been added no further back than from one of her grandparents.

She was entirely white, and as gaunt as the man. Her winter coat had come in, full, bushy, and spotless, which rounded off the sharpest angles of her boniness. The plume of her tail flowed forward, flat along her back, nearly to the shoulder. Her feet were compact and round, with closely-bunched toes. The breadth of skull between her ears gave space for a brain. Her eyes were deeply inset, within the oblique cracks that converged upon her muzzle. Her bone structure was massive, deep in the chest, strong in the foreleg, rectangular in the outline of the body. Ears erect, she watched the strangers' approach, moving to a position between her owner and them, in a gesture that combined dignity with protection.

191

The man seemed to be in a coma, and did not raise his head. Plainly his first need was food. With half an eye the boys could see that he was starving. Bringing out their lunch, Sandy held a sandwich to the stranger's lips. Weak as he was, the man's teeth tore into the bread and bacon, not waiting to chew between gulps. Sandy knew that people far gone with hunger must be fed often and but little at a time, and gave him no more.

Meantime Beaver had been examining the man's possessions, which were meagre enough—a rifle, the remnant of a blanket, a frying pan and his knapsack. Rummaging in the knapsack, he held up two cartridges.

"You take the rifle, Beaver," said Sandy. "You are the best hunter. Get a rabbit or a bird, if you can, while I remake the fire."

As Sandy pawed dry moss together and broke off dead branches, the man was trying to disengage something from inside his shirt. Tied against his ribs was a packet wrapped in oiled skin. His voice was gone, but he motioned for Sandy to open it and read. Inside were newspaper clippings and certificates testifying that Horace Manton had been the winner, on three successive years of the Nome Gold Cup Race.

Before Sandy had spelled out the sense of the papers and had teased the smudge into a blaze, Little Beaver was back with a snowshoe hare. He skinned it—tossing the head, feet, pelt and insides to the dog—cut it in small pieces, filled the fry-pan with water at the spring, and set

192

the mixture upon the fire. While it was bubbling Sandy fed the man half of a second sandwich. Once the meat was tender and somewhat cooled, Sandy knelt behind Mr. Manton, supporting him in a sitting position, while Little Beaver tilted the pan, letting the liquid trickle between his lips. The man's strength was reviving. He opened his eyes and whispered a few words of thanks. The boys had arrived in the nick of time, at the very moment the Old Racer was fading into unconsciousness.

For a couple of hours they busied themselves around the lean-to. Mrs. Mackay had prepared four sandwiches for each of them, but they contented themselves with a piece of rabbit and a single sandwich apiece. They gave the dog one sandwich, the bones, and the pan to lick. The rest of the meat and the remaining bread and bacon they rolled in the knapsack, warning the man that he was to save it for supper. They washed the pan at the spring, filled it with fresh water, and left it within reach, in case he should be thirsty. Sandy peeled off the light parka that he wore over his shirt, and worked it down over the shoulders of his patient.

"Are you sure that you don't want to come along with us?" he asked.

The old man shook his head, and pointed at the dog, as if that were answer enough.

"Tomorrow is Sunday," Sandy said. "No school. We'll be back early. Nothing will trouble you tonight with that dog on guard. What do you call her?"

193

The Old Racer's face lighted with pleasure. "Ne-Nu-Ka," he breathed hoarsely. The boys grinned. They liked the name and repeated it to themselves. A good name for a good dog.

As the day waned, one of the autumn fogs that prevail in the Hudson Bay country was closing in. Near the man's hand, the boys piled such dry wood as they could gather without an axe, threw fresh evergreens upon the roof of the lean-to, and others upon the ground for a bed. For the time being it was all that they could do. The Old Racer raised his hand in salute as they left. The dog stood like a white statue in the mist.

Each day thereafter for a month, one or both of the boys visited Calico Spring. At first the man gained strength and even took short strolls. The improvement, however, was temporary. It might be some illness, or it might be simply the effect of prolonged underfeeding and overexertion, but after a fortnight each visit found him a trifle weaker. He did not complain, nor was he in pain. His memory was a screen, across which marched the events of his tumultuous career. He talked incessantly, sensible talk, thrilling talk, priceless talk about the one thing of importance to him—the training and racing of dogs. He knew that he was soon to embark upon his last journey, and so held back no secret.

And, fact by fact, the fantastic narrative of the Old Racer's wanderings was woven together. Ne-Nu-Ka had had a mate, the lead dog of Manton's winning team in the second and third Nome Races. For his purity of color and his thistledown lightness of foot, he had been known throughout the Yukon as the White Phantom. At the apex of his fame he had returned to the wild. It might have been the wanderlust of the wolf blood. It might have been the attraction of a new mate.

Without his unmatched leader, Manton lost faith in his team. He determined to get him back or to perish in the quest. With a twelve-dog hitch and a full sledge of food, he had plotted a course where the white packs range. Always hopeful, always on the look-out, man and team had gone on and on. Supplies were consumed. The team went lame, sickened, dropped out. At the end, on foot, with his rifle and the white female, Manton battled on alone.

Strange to believe, the lost one had been found. But by the irony of circumstances, when the White Phantom rejoined his master and his abandoned mate, he was in as wretched a condition as they. Manton found him one morning, lying beside Ne-Nu-Ka, licking his wounds. He had evidently been mangled by some younger leader, who had ousted him from the leadership of the pack.

The goal of his search having been attained, the Old Racer now set out for the habitations of men. Meekly the Phantom had followed, taking his third of such game as his owner could bring down. But the love of battle still beat in his pulse. Injured as he was, he had rushed into a band of night skulkers. They were too strong and too

195

many for him. Daybreak found what was left of him stark and cold.

The Racer had the Northlander's wholesome respect for the alder marshes, and although it took him far out of his desired course, he had made the circuit of them. With the last dregs of his strength he had built his fire near the banks of the Abitibi, ignorant of Porcupine's nearness.

But even more fascinating to the boys than the Old Racer's story was the knowledge he poured out to them. He described how to choose dogs for speed and for stamina, how to doctor feet sore from ice, slush, or gravel, how to groom and feed animals during a race, what harness would tire them the least. With minute care he named the qualities of the natural-born lead-dog, the points that would make him the better half of any team. Summoning Ne-Nu-Ka, he would demonstrate upon her body the marks of the prime sledge animal, the ample brain chamber, the muscled haunches that pushed forward the load, the four white stockings that were his own pet superstition.

The man's voice vibrated, his eye brightened, he forgot the hopeless squalor of his position, as he again lived his triumphs. The boys would sit before the lean-to, breathless, hugging their knees, under a magician's spell. They realized that these were lessons from a great master of his art. They must be memorized, each sentence of this concentrated wisdom. For the sled dog is man's best

Injured as he was, the White Phantom had rushed into a
band of night skulkers

197

friend in the North Country. He can haul as much as a man can haul, but he can haul it sixty miles a day instead of fifteen. And the man who knows dogs has precious knowledge.

The old man was fondly insistent in explaining the systems for attaching freight dogs to a komatik or sled. The styles of harness, said he, and the names applied to them, differ according to the region, according to the temperament of the driver. When a number of animals, however, are to be tied to a sled for the purpose of pulling it, it is inevitably done in one of three ways: by using the fan hitch, in which each dog has a separate and independent tugline to the sled, and in which, as the name implies, the animals when in motion spread out like the ribs of a fan; or by using the single line tandem hitch, in which the animals, singly, and on alternate sides, are snapped to the tow or truck line; or by using the swing hitch, in which the animals are paired, side by side, like a team of horses, and the tugline passes between them, like the pole of a wagon.

The fan hitch, said the Old Racer, has three advantages, which is why numbers of Indians and Eskimos employ it. On rough surfaces it permits the dogs to spread out and each can choose his own path. Should an accident occur, such as a snow slide, or an unexpected crack in the ice, with one slash of his knife the driver can cut loose each dog from the sled and from every other dog. Each is given a chance to save himself. This is also an advantage

 198

if a caribou or polar bear is sighted, for the dog team can instantly become a hunting pack. In the fan hitch, too, the members of the team are spread out before the driver. He can tell which are soldiering, and ply his whip accordingly. But in this hitch there is a waste of team energy, as the dogs on the flanks expend much of their power pulling to the right or to the left, rather than pulling straight ahead.

The single line hitch is simple, and if dogs are new to the work or quarrelsome it gives more scope to the individual, who can, without hitting another dog, pass from one side of the tugline to the other, and shift the pressure of the collar on his neck. The tandem hitch is ideal for narrow trails, along which the single file of dogs can weave like a snake.

In the hitch by pairs, the couples are called swings, and the team will be composed of four or more swings, plus the leader. As the leader is supposed to guide rather than to haul, he is frequently tied on a free line, well out in front of the first swing. This free line helps him to turn a heavy team when they are moving fast, and if it is long enough he may even turn and bark in the faces of his team-mates, to bring them to a quicker halt. The Old Racer himself always used the swing hitch, which had been invented by one of his friends. Once the dogs know their work, and are acquainted with each other, this hitch makes for cooperation and team spirit.

The dimensions of the komatik and the words of com-

199

mand, said the Old Racer, vary in different localities, just as do the types of harness. The main consideration is for each driver to work out the system under which his dogs handle best. For his own sledge the Racer preferred a solid framework of oak, 24 inches wide and 10 feet long, with runners shod with iron, and projecting 18 inches beyond the upright rear wall.

The four or five command words used for the team should be distinctive and easily distinguished. They may be in any language, or mere arbitrary sounds. But as each word represents a concrete action on the part of the leader and team, sounds should be chosen which hit the ear with a sharp impact. In his own driving vocabulary, Mr. Manton had borrowed the starting signal of the Siberians, a series of high rolling R's, "P-r-r-r-r-h. Prrrrrh." To halt he employed the French Canadian phrase, "Array," shortened form of arretez. For the turn to the right, "Gee," and the turn to the left, "Haw," he used the terms that ox drivers and teamsters have shouted to their plow teams time out of mind. The four sounds differed so radically that there was no danger of the dogs mistaking one for another.

Out of his experience the Old Racer advised the precaution of a stop line, and of a metal bar to serve as a brake. The stop line, a cord or strap fifty feet long, drags behind the sled. Should a driver, running beside his team, sprain an ankle, or, riding on the rear extensions of the runner, slip off, he can grab the stop line as he falls and bring the team to a halt. Mr. Manton had harrowing tales of the fate of the drivers who had fallen and were obliged to watch their food, their weapons, and their homeward racing dogs disappear over the horizon. It is always better practice for two men to go with a team, or for two teams to travel in company. Of these and of every matter pertaining to the work dog, did the old expert unburden himself. The boys brought him food for the body, and he repaid them with food for the imagination and the mind.

It was a month since the Racer's appearance, and the winter freeze-up was already due. Bringing the daily basket of food, Sandy and Beaver had hard work paddling against the icy wind that swept down the river. Fifty feet from the lean-to the dog was whining softly to herself. The old man, features composed, did not stir. He had died, then, as he had wished, in the solitude of the bush, with the companionship of his dog. She raised her muzzle in the grief song of the tundra. You-oo-oo-oo. You-oo-oo-ooh. Evidently he had known that the end was coming, for at his side, held by a stone, was a message for the boys. "I leave you Ne-Nu-Ka. It is a great gift. Save all her puppies. White Phantom is their father. The runt of the litter, keep him too. Do this without fail. The rifle is for Beaver."

He had already told them what to do with his body. Silently they tied against his heart the packet that told of his glories as a racer, wound him in his blanket, and carried the bundle to the stream. The current took it quietly.

201

They called the dog. She was theirs now, but with her they had accepted the death-bed obligation to rear all the puppies that were soon to be born. Especially the pee-wee of the litter, which dog-breeders usually suppress. That was hard to understand.

At a distance the dog followed. She paused, looking first to the north, then at the boys, as though balancing the two futures. Should her fate be with the free animals of the north, or should it be with man? She refused to enter the canoe, or even to come near it. But when the boys reached the other side she was waiting for them. She had made her choice and had thrown in her lot with man.

Eight of them, there were, and all beauties. Four were entirely white, like their parents; two had black heads and necks; one was a tortoise-shell, yellow, black and white; the eighth puppy was the runt, the midget of the family. He was coal black save for a white star on the chest and a comic pink nose. The boys remembered what the Old Racer had written about keeping them all, and taking good care of the runt. They called the little one Quicksilver. He was the first to bark. The whole litter would be lying peacefully at breakfast, or lunch. They were busy and would not bother to look up at the footsteps of strangers. That is, all except the runt. He would leave the dinner table, brace himself on his four wobbly legs, and yip-yip his defiance.

On the fifth day, after a deal of low-voiced discussion,

the boys performed a ceremony. They christened the pups with a secret mark. "All the dogs we shall ever own must have that mark," they agreed. "We want something that people won't notice, and yet something that we ourselves can discover at once. Dogs have a way of getting lost and stolen, when they become useful. This way there will be no fight over ownership." The private mark was a nick on the inner edge of the left ear. Ne-Nu-Ka bared her teeth when the first pup whimpered, but after that she licked away the tiny drops of blood and all was calm. Within the week the hair had grown and covered the small cuts.

The big problem, however, was food. If they were to be heavy, whipcord creatures like their mother, if some were even to have the speed and stamina of the famous White Phantom, Ne-Nu-Ka must be fed all the seal meat and corn meal mush that she could swallow. But that would be merely for the first seven weeks. Afterward there would be nine mouths, to be filled with bumper rations twice in the day. Adult dogs, even when working severely, are fed but once in 24 hours, but growing pups develop better on a morning and a night feeding.

As it was mid-winter there was no regular supply of fish. But seal could be captured by an experienced hunter. This is where Chief Big Beaver's skill was of immense help. The seal used to be a land animal, he explained, and is still an air-breather. During frozen weather it must keep airholes open with its teeth, even when the ice is thickest. Every thirty minutes the seal pushes his nose into the open air for another breath. Big Beaver would locate the breathing-spots by tracing the tracks of wolves. There he waited with poised harpoons, speared the seal in the head, chopped away the ice, and pulled forth the prize. But it required practice, a lightning quick hand, and a sure eye.

There was also the matter of a house for the dogs. To meet the emergency of the puppies' birth they had driven small logs, sharpened at one end, into the snow, forming a circle, with a gap on the south side for a door. The logs to the north were shorter, thus giving a slant to the roof of evergreen boughs that were thickly piled across the top. This made a good enough make-shift for freezing weather. But when the snow melted the house would tumble in. No, they needed a substantial year-round house, and they needed fencing to make a runway, and cash to buy two seals a week.

Corporal Donaldson, whom they encountered return-ing on snowshoes from one of his lonely patrols had an idea which he promised to follow up that very evening. On his radio he often caught oddments of news which might be turned to account. And, as a matter of fact, it was through this channel that the boys eventually landed their cash-paying work.

"It's this way," related the Corporal, three mornings later. "The Paper Company has bought that valley of young spruce twenty miles south, on the railway line. They are starting to cut at once. They will pile the pulp

204

wood, in four-foot lengths, alongside the track, and haul it out when the trains get to running again. They want cutters. It's light work, soft wood, and they want logs not over eight inches through at the butt. You don't need to peel it. And you get board and $2.35 a cord, piled where it falls. Looks to me like a job made to order for you boys."

"But who would look after the dogs?" Sandy asked.

Corporal Don considered. "What about Bumbly Bill's Sally?"

At the other end of Three-Mile Trail lived Bumbly Bill, the one-armed station master, with his wife Celeste and their seven children. Sally, the oldest, was twelve, and literally her father's right hand. But now that train service was over until spring, Sally's duties were lighter. Although a girl, she was capable, self-reliant, and entirely trustworthy. It was a good suggestion, and the boys set out for Bumbly Bill's forthwith.

Sally was delighted at the prospect of ready cash. For fifty cents a day she agreed to walk the three miles to the Factory, feed the dogs, and look after their well being. It was the beginning of a most satisfactory business arrangement.

On their return from the wood cutting, the boys walked with a slight swagger. They had been out in the world, for a trial flight. Each of them had taken five dollars spending money for himself. They paid two dollars for the rent of the cross-cut saw and for files, and they had

205

forty-three dollars salted away in the Company's safe, for wire fencing, hardware and corn meal. Sally had done her work well. The pups were running about, jolly as woolly muffs. And young as they were, they were tramping nests in the snow, in which to fold their tails over their noses and snooze. Although Ne-Nu-Ka had weaned her children and had apparently washed her paws of further responsibility, she was still very much the head of the family, as she was soon to prove.

Bordering the establishment of the Hudson's Bay Company upon the river bank, stood the store of Butcher Smok, formerly a trapper employed by the Company, who had set himself up as a rival fur buyer. He was a blond giant, proud that no razor had ever touched his face, the son of a Norwegian sailor and an Ojibway squaw. On whaling ships and on Grand Banks fishing smacks, in logging camps, in trapland scuffles, he had kicked and gouged his way to leadership.

Combining the forest cunning of his mother with the cold daring of his father, for twenty years Butch had been a better-than-ordinary trapper. But his success as a fighter had turned his head. Being the hero of scores of Indian and Eskimo villages out-balanced his good sense. He conceived the idea that the Company manager, John Mackay, was cheating him on prices.

In Butch's one-track mind, to conceive of a grievance was to act on it, and Porcupine still remembered the

206

morning when, in a store full of customers, his anger had exploded in wild words and flying fists. With outstretched arms he had defied the world. His lion's mane combed erect by clawing fingers, his nose hammered flat, one ear half bitten off, his beard a tangle of blood and tobacco, a dozen arms had dragged him from the Company store, more dead than alive. But he was a fighter to the end. Regaining consciousness, he had re-entered the store, leaped upon a counter, and in the presence of thirty men, sworn a hair-curling oath to get square with the Company. To make good that oath had been the objective of his life since that day. He had hewn himself a three-room store and dwelling just south of the Company property. And in the dozen years that had intervened he had never been known to forsake his twin principles—to be a friend to his friends, and to be an enemy of the Company. His great rolling laugh could be heard up and down the river, as he welcomed customers to his landing-stage.

A group of wholesale grocers and clothiers, back in the cities, impressed by his twenty-year record as a successful trapper, as well as by his wife's kinship with influential Ojibway chiefs, furnished him a stock of merchandise on credit. With the rising price of fur, Butch paid off his debts and doubled his stock.

In Pete, Butch had a dog after his own heart. Scarred by battles with every breed of dog or wolf that entered the North Country, the iron-grey mongrel was half boar-

207

hound and half mastiff. His temper was such that even Butch judged it better that he be chained during business hours.

But on the last morning of his life, either by ill-will or by mistake, Pete was left untied. Monarch of all he surveyed, he had made the tour of his master's warehouse, and now stood regarding the expanse of river and field, hoping that he might see something with which he could quarrel. He had not long to wait.

Quicksilver, puppy explorer, runt of the litter, had eaten heartily and was keen to learn more of the universe. Disgusted with his stick-in-the-mud brothers, he trotted out in front of the Company's store and barked. He saw the big slate-gray dog and advanced to make friends.

Pete dropped on his haunches, ears alert. The puppy would walk straight into his mouth. Pete's red tongue licked his lips. This was going to be good. For the dog hated the Company and its creatures, downrightly as did his master.

But in the split second before the great hound seized the puppy, a blur of white raced from behind the Company's store. Straight as a bullet she covered the hundred yards. Pete, hypnotized, watched her shoulder the pup aside, watched her dive at himself. Ne-Nu-Ka knew the hold she was after and did not miss her calculation. She was under the boarhound's body, her teeth fastened upon the shoulder joint of his opposite foreleg. Her head was between Pete's front legs, her eyes and throat pushing

208

against and protected by his throat, her body slinking to the rear, parallel to his own, and nimbly out of reach of the slashing mastiff teeth.

Once Ne-Nu-Ka had settled to her hold, it would hardly be the truth to call it a fight. His attempts to break loose from her grip not succeeding, Pete went stark, staring mad. He rolled, he leaped, he threw himself backward. But always that white body turned as he turned, just out of reach. Always that grip was boring into his shoulder, implacable as a bear trap.

Hearing the rumpus, Sandy and Beaver had run up from their kennel, and stood rooted to the spot. Butch himself came out of his store, and stood on the platform, arms akimbo, a snarl on his lips. He re-entered the building and returned with a rifle.

"Call off y'r sneak-fightin' cur," he shouted to Sandy. "That ain't no fair-fightin' dog. Call her off, 'r I'll shoot the two o' them."

Ne-Nu-Ka was persuaded to let go. Warily she made a circle to the rear, on guard against the man as much as against his dog. Butch walked carelessly over to Pete, who stopped licking his foreleg and raised his head apologetically. The big man rested the muzzle of the rifle between his dog's eyes and fired twice.

"I don't want no dog, n'r no nuthin', belongin' t'me, what ain't a champion. 'N you keep y'r eye peeled f'r the next watch dog I get me. Y' ain't seen nuthin' yet."

The boys were deep in thought as they followed Ne-

209

Nu-Ka and the chastened Quicksilver back to her kennel. Their respect for the dog had gone up a hundred points. Indeed, the Old Racer had given them a monumental legacy. Behind Ne-Nu-Ka's golden eyes lay instincts better than a brain. With Pete's whole body to choose from, she had dived unerringly for the one foolproof spot. She had done it like a professional, with no fumbling, no uncertainty. Surely she had practiced these holds before. Sandy felt a prickle of pride between his shoulder blades.

"Some dog," he murmured.

Beaver grunted approvingly.

The Coming of Lad

by ALBERT PAYSON TERHUNE

In the mile-away village of Hampton, there had been a veritable epidemic of burglaries—ranging from the theft of a brand-new ash-can from the steps of the Methodist chapel to the ravaging of Mrs. Blauvelt's whole lineful of clothes, on a washday dusk.

Up the Valley and down it, from Tuxedo to Ridgewood, there had been a half-score robberies of a very different order—depredations wrought, manifestly by professionals; thieves whose motor cars served the twentieth century purpose of such historic steeds as Dick Turpin's Black Bess and Jack Shepard's Ranter. These thefts were in the line of jewelry and the like; and were as daringly wrought as were the modest local operators' raids on ash-can and laundry.

It is the easiest thing in the world to stir humankind's ever-tense burglar-nerves into hysterical jangling. In house after house, for miles of the peaceful North Jersey

This story is from THE HEART OF A DOG, by Albert Payson Terhune

211

region, old pistols were cleaned and loaded; window fastenings and door-locks were inspected and new hiding-places found for portable family treasures.

Across the lake from the village, and down the Valley from a dozen country homes, seeped the tide of precautions. And it swirled at last around the Place,—a thirty-acre homestead, isolated and sweet, whose grounds ran from highway to lake; and whose wisteria-clad grey house drowsed among big oaks midway between road and water; a furlong or more distant from either.

The Place's family dog,—a pointer,—had died, rich in years and honour. And the new peril of burglary made it highly needful to choose a successor for him.

The Master talked of buying a whalebone-and-steel-and-snow bull terrier, or a more formidable if more greedy Great Dane. But the Mistress wanted a collie. So they compromised by getting the collie.

He reached the Place in a crampy and smelly crate; preceded by a long envelope containing an intricate and imposing pedigree. The burglary-preventing problem seemed solved.

But when the crate was opened and its occupant stepped gravely forth, on the Place's veranda, the problem was revived.

All the Master and the Mistress had known about the newcomer,—apart from his price and his lofty lineage,—was that his breeder had named him "Lad."

From these meagre facts they had somehow built up a

212

picture of a huge and grimly ferocious animal that should be a terror to all intruders and that might in time be induced to make friends with the Place's vouched-for occupants. In view of this, they had had a stout kennel made and to it they had affixed with double staples a chain strong enough to restrain a bull.

(It may as well be said here that never in all the sixteen years of his beautiful life did Lad occupy that or any other kennel nor wear that or any other chain.)

Even the crate which brought the new dog to the Place failed somehow to destroy the illusion of size and fierceness. But, the moment the crate door was opened the delusion was wrecked by Lad himself.

Out on to the porch he walked. The ramshackle crate behind him had a ridiculous air of a chrysalis from which some bright thing had departed. For a shaft of sunlight was shimmering athwart the veranda floor. And into the middle of the warm bar of radiance Laddie stepped,— and stood.

His fluffy puppy-coat of wavy mahogany-and-white caught a million sunbeams, reflecting them back in tawny-orange glints and in a dazzle as of snow. His forepaws were absurdly small, even for a puppy's. Above them the ridging of the stocky legbones gave as clear promise of mighty size and strength as did the amazingly deep little chest and square shoulders.

Here one day would stand a giant among dogs, powerful as a timber-wolf, lithe as a cat, as dangerous to foes as

213

an angry tiger; a dog without fear or treachery; a dog of uncanny brain and great lovingly loyal heart and, withal, a dancing sense of fun. A dog with a soul.

All this, any canine physiologist might have read from the compact frame, the proud head-carriage, the smoulder in the deep-set sorrowful dark eyes. To the casual observer, he was but a beautiful and appealing and wonderfully cuddleable bunch of puppy-hood.

Lad's dark eyes swept the porch, the soft swelling green of the lawn, the flash of fire-blue lake among the trees below. Then, he deigned to look at the group of humans at one side of him. Gravely, impersonally, he surveyed them; not at all cowed or strange in his new surroundings; courteously inquisitive as to the twist of luck that had set him down here and as to the people who, presumably, were to be his future companions.

Perhaps the stout little heart quivered just a bit, if memory went back to his home kennel and to the rowdy throng of brothers and sisters, and most of all, to the soft furry mother against whose side he had nestled every night since he was born. But if so, Lad was too valiant to show homesickness by so much as a whimper. And, assuredly, this House of Peace was infinitely better than the miserable crate wherein he had spent twenty horrible and jouncing and smelly and noisy hours.

From one to another of the group strayed the level sorrowful gaze. After the swift inspection, Laddie's eyes rested again on the Mistress. For an instant, he

214

stood, looking at her, in that mildly polite curiosity which held no hint of personal interest.

Then, all at once, his plumy tail began to wave. Into his sad eyes sprang a flicker of warm friendliness. Unbidden —oblivious of every one else—he trotted across to where the Mistress sat. He put one tiny white paw in her lap; and stood thus, looking up lovingly into her face, tail awag, eyes shining.

"There's no question whose dog he's going to be," laughed the Master. "He's elected you,—by acclamation."

The Mistress caught up into her arms the half-grown youngster, petting his silken head, running her white fingers through his shining mahogany coat; making crooning little friendly noises to him. Lad forgot he was a dignified and stately pocket-edition of a collie. Under this spell, he changed in a second to an excessively loving and nestling and adoring puppy.

"Just the same," interposed the Master, "we've been stung. I wanted a dog to guard the Place and to be a menace to burglars and all that sort of thing. And they've sent us a Teddy-Bear. I think I'll ship him back and get a grown one. What sort of use is—?"

"He is going to be all those things," eagerly prophesied the Mistress. "And a hundred more. See how he loves to have me pet him! And,—look—he's learned, already, to shake hands, and—"

"Fine!" applauded the Master. "So when it comes our turn to be visited by this motor-Raffles, the puppy will

215

shake hands with him, and register love of petting; and the burly marauder will be so touched by Lad's friendliness that he'll not only spare our house but lead an upright life ever after. I—"

"Don't send him back!" she pleaded. "He'll grow up, soon, and—"

"And if only the courteous burglars will wait till he's a couple of years old," suggested the Master, "he—"

Set gently on the floor by the Mistress, Laddie had crossed to where the Master stood. The man, glancing down, met the puppy's gaze. For an instant he scowled at the miniature watchdog, so ludicrously different from the ferocious brute he had expected. Then,—for some queer reason,—he stooped and ran his hand roughly over the tawny coat, letting it rest at last on the shapely head that did not flinch or wriggle at his touch.

"All right," he decreed. "Let him stay. He'll be an amusing pet for you, anyhow. And his eye has the true thoroughbred expression,—'the look of eagles.' He may amount to something after all. Let him stay. We'll take a chance on burglars."

So it was that Lad came to the Place. So it was that he demanded and received due welcome;—which was ever Lad's way. The Master had been right about the pup's proving "an amusing pet," for the Mistress. From that first hour, Lad was never willingly out of her sight. He had adopted her. The Master, too,—in only a little lesser wholeheartedness,—he adopted. Toward the rest of the

216

world, from the first, he was friendly but more or less in-different.

Almost at once, his owners noted an odd trait in the dog's nature. He would of course get into any or all of the thousand mischief-scrapes which are the heritage of puppies. But, a single reproof was enough to cure him forever of the particular form of mischief which had just been chidden. He was one of those rare dogs that learn the law by instinct; and that remember for all time a command or a prohibition once given them.

For example:—On his second day at the Place, he made a furious rush at a neurotic mother hen and her golden convoy of chicks. The Mistress,—luckily for all concerned,—was within call. At her sharp summons the puppy wheeled, midway in his charge, and trotted back to her. Severely, yet trying not to laugh at his worried aspect, she scolded Lad for his misdeed.

An hour later, as Lad was scampering ahead of her, past the stables, they rounded a corner and came flush upon the same nerve-wracked hen and her brood. Lad halted in his scamper, with a suddenness that made him skid. Then, walking as though on eggs, he made an idiotically wide circle about the feathered dam and her silly chicks. Never thereafter did he assail any of the Place's fowls.

It was the same, when he sprang up merrily at a line of laundry, flapping an alluring invitation from the drying ground lines. A single word of rebuke,—and thenceforth the family wash was safe from him.

217

And so on with the myriad perplexing "Don'ts" which spatter the career of a fun-loving collie pup. Versed in the patience-fraying ways of pups in general, the Mistress and the Master marvelled and bragged and praised.

All day and every day, life was a delight to the little dog. He had friends everywhere, willing to romp with him. He had squirrels to chase, among the oaks. He had the lake to splash ecstatically in. He had all he wanted to eat; and he had all the petting his hungry little heart could crave.

He was even allowed, with certain restrictions, to come into the mysterious house itself. Nor, after one defiant bark at a leopardskin rug, did he molest anything therein. In the house, too, he found a genuine cave:—a wonderful place to lie and watch the world at large, and to stay cool in and to pretend he was a wolf. The cave was the deep space beneath the piano in the music room. It seemed to have a peculiar charm to Lad. To the end of his days, by the way, this cave was his chosen resting place. Nor, in his lifetime, did any other dog set foot therein.

So much for "all day and every day." But the nights were different.

Lad hated the nights. In the first place, everybody went to bed and left him alone. In the second, his hard-hearted owners made him sleep on a fluffy rug in a corner of the veranda instead of in his delectable piano-cave. Moreover, there was no food at night. And there was nobody to play with or to go for walks with or to listen to. There was nothing but gloom and silence and dullness.

When a puppy takes fifty cat-naps in the course of the day, he cannot always be expected to sleep the night through. It is too much to ask. And Lad's waking hours at night were times of desolation and of utter boredom. True, he might have consoled himself, as does many a lesser pup, with voicing his woes in a series of melancholy howls. That, in time, would have drawn plenty of human attention to the lonely youngster; even if the attention were not wholly flattering.

But Lad did not belong to the howling type. When he was unhappy, he waxed silent. And his sorrowful eyes took on a deeper woe. By the way, if there is anything more sorrowful than the eyes of a collie pup that has never known sorrow, I have yet to see it.

No, Lad could not howl. And he could not hunt for squirrels. For these enemies of his were not content with the unsportsmanliness of climbing out of his reach in the daytime, when he chased them; but they added to their sins by joining the rest of the world,—except Lad,— in sleeping all night. Even the lake that was so friendly by day was a chilly and forbidding playfellow on the cool North Jersey nights.

There was nothing for a poor lonely pup to do but stretch out on his rug and stare in unhappy silence up the driveway, in the impossible hope that some one might happen along through the darkness to play with him.

219

At such an hour and in such lonesomeness, Lad would gladly have tossed aside all prejudices of caste,—and all his natural dislikes,—and would have frolicked in mad joy with the veriest stranger. Anything was better than this drear solitude throughout the million hours before the first of the maids should be stirring or the first of the farmhands report for work. Yes, night was a disgusting time; and it had not one single redeeming trait for the puppy.

Lad was not even consoled by the knowledge that he was guarding the slumbrous house. He was not guarding it. He had not the very remotest idea what it meant to be a watchdog. In all his five months he had never learned that there is unfriendliness in the world; or that there is anything to guard a house against.

True, it was instinctive with him to bark when people came down the drive, or appeared at the gates without warning. But more than once the Master had bidden him be silent when a rackety puppy salvo of barking had broken in on the arrival of some guest. And Lad was still in perplexed doubt as to whether barking was something forbidden or merely limited.

One night,—a solemn, black, breathless August night, when half-visible heat lightning turned the murk of the western horizon to pulses of dirty sulphur,—Lad awoke from a fitful dream of chasing squirrels which had never learned to climb.

He sat up on his rug, blinking around through the

220

gloom in the half hope that some of those non-climbing squirrels might still be in sight. As they were not, he sighed unhappily and prepared to lay his classic young head back again on the rug for another spell of night-shortening sleep.

But before his head could touch the rug, he reared it and half of his small body from the floor and focused his nearsighted eyes on the driveway. At the same time, his tail began to wag a thumping welcome.

Now, by day, a dog cannot see so far nor so clearly as can a human. But at night,—for comparatively short distances,—he can see much better than can his master. By day or by darkness, his keen hearing and keener scent make up for all defects of eyesight.

And now three of Lad's senses told him he was no longer alone in his tedious vigil. Down the drive, moving with amusing slowness and silence, a man was coming. He was on foot. And he was fairly well dressed. Dogs,—the foremost snobs in creation,—are quick to note the difference between a well-clad and a disreputable stranger.

Here unquestionably was a visitor:—some such man as so often came to the Place and paid such flattering attention to the puppy. No longer need Lad be bored by the solitude of this particular night. Some one was coming towards the house and carrying a small bag under his arm. Some one to make friends with. Lad was very happy.

Deep in his throat a welcoming bark was born. But he stilled it. Once, when he had barked at the approach of a

221

stranger, the stranger had gone away. If this stranger were to go away, all the night's fun would go with him. Also, no later than yesterday, the Master had scolded Lad for barking at a man who had called. Wherefore the dog held his peace.

Getting to his feet and stretching himself, fore and aft, in true collie fashion, the pup gambolled up the drive to meet the visitor.

The man was feeling his way through the pitch darkness, groping cautiously; halting once or twice for a smoulder of lightning to silhouette the house he was nearing. In a wooded lane, a quarter mile away, his lightless motor car waited.

Lad trotted up to him, the tiny white feet noiseless in the soft dust of the drive. The man did not see him, but passed so close to the dog's hospitably upthrust nose that he all but touched it.

Only slightly rebuffed at such chill lack of cordiality, Lad fell in behind him, tail awag, and followed him to the porch. When the guest should ring the bell, the Master or one of the maids would come to the door. There would be lights and talk; and perhaps Laddie himself might be allowed to slip in to his beloved cave.

But the man did not ring. He did not stop at the door, at all. On tiptoe he skirted the veranda to the old-fashioned bay windows at the south side of the living room;—windows with catches as old-fashioned and as simple to open as themselves.

222

Lad padded along, a pace or so to the rear;—still hopeful of being petted or perhaps even romped with. The man gave a faint but promising sign of intent to romp, by swinging his small and very shiny brown bag to and fro as he walked. Thus ever did the Master swing Lad's precious canton flannel doll before throwing it for him to retrieve. Lad made a tentative snap at the bag, his tail wagging harder than ever. But he missed it. And, in another moment the man stopped swinging the bag and tucked it under his arm again as he began to fumble with a bit of steel.

There was the very faintest of clicks. Then, noiselessly the window slid upward. A second fumbling sent the wooden inside shutters ajar. The man worked with no uncertainty. Ever since his visit to the Place, a week earlier, behind the aegis of a big and bright and newly forged telephone-inspector badge, he had carried in his trained memory the location of windows and of obstructing furniture and of the primitive small safe in the living room wall, with its pitifully pickable lock;—the safe wherein the Place's few bits of valuable jewelry and other compact treasures reposed at night.

Lad was tempted to follow the creeping body and the fascinatingly swinging bag indoors. But his one effort to enter the house,—with muddy paws,—by way of an open window, had been rebuked by the Lawgivers. He had been led to understand that really well-bred little dogs come in by way of the door; and then only on permission.

223

So he waited, doubtfully, at the veranda edge; in the hope that his new friend might reappear or that the Master might perhaps want to show off his pup to the caller, as so often the Master was wont to do.

Head cocked to one side, tulip ears alert, Laddie stood listening. To the keenest human ears the thief's soft progress across the wide living room to the wall-safe would have been all but inaudible. But Lad could follow every phase of it;—the cautious skirting of each chair; the hesitant pause as a bit of ancient furniture creaked; the halt in front of the safe; the queer grinding noise, muffled but persevering, at the lock; then the faint creak of the swinging iron door, and the deft groping of fingers.

Soon, the man started back toward the paler oblong of gloom which marked the window's outlines from the surrounding black. Lad's tail began to wag again. Apparently, this eccentric person was coming out, after all, to keep him company. Now, the man was kneeling on the window-seat. Now, in gingerly fashion, he reached forward and set the small bag down on the veranda; before negotiating the climb across the broad seat,—a climb that might well call for the use of both his hands.

Lad was entranced. Here was a game he understood. Thus, more than once, had the Mistress tossed out to him his flannel doll, as he had stood in pathetic invitation on the porch, looking in at her as she read or talked. She had laughed at his wild tossings and other maltreatments

 224

of the limp doll. He had felt he was scoring a real hit. And this hit he decided to repeat.

Snatching up the swollen little satchel, almost before it left the intruder's hand, Lad shook it, joyously, revelling in the faint clink and jingle of the contents. He backed playfully away; the bag-handle swinging in his jaws. Crouching low, he wagged his tail in ardent invitation to the stranger to chase him and to get back the satchel. Thus did the Master romp with Lad when the flannel doll was the prize of their game. And Lad loved such races.

Yes, the stranger was accepting the invitation. The moment he had crawled out on the veranda he reached down for the bag. As it was not where he thought he had left it, he swung his groping hand forward in a half-circle, his finger sweeping the floor.

Make that enticing motion, directly in front of a playful collie pup;—especially if he has something he doesn't want you to take from him;—and watch the effect.

Instantly, Lad was athrill with the spirit of the game. In one scurrying backward jump, he was off the veranda and on the lawn, tail vibrating, eyes dancing; satchel held tantalisingly toward its would-be possessor.

The light sound of his body touching ground reached the man. Reasoning that the sweep of his own arm had somehow knocked the bag off the porch, he ventured off the edge of the veranda and flashed a swathed ray of his pocket light along the ground in search of it.

225

The flashlight's lens was cleverly muffled; in a way to give forth but a single subdued finger of illumination. That one brief glimmer was enough to show the thief a right impossible sight. The glow struck answering lights from the polished sides of the brown bag. The bag was hanging in air some six inches above the grass and perhaps five feet away from him. Then he saw it swing frivolously to one side and vanish in the night.

The astonished man had seen more. Feeble was the flashlight's shrouded ray—too feeble to outline against the night the small dark body behind the shining brown bag. But that same ray caught and reflected back to the incredulous beholder two splashes of pale fire;—glints from a pair of deep-set collie-eyes.

As the bag disappeared, the eerie fire-points were gone. The thief all but dropped his flashlight. He gaped in nervous dread; and sought vainly to account for the witchwork he had witnessed.

He had plenty of nerve. He had plenty of experience along his chosen line of endeavour. But while a crook may control his nerve, he cannot make it phlegmatic or steady. Always, he must be conscious of holding it in check, as a clever driver checks and steadies and keeps in subjection a plunging horse. Let the vigilance slacken, and there is a runaway.

Now this particular marauder had long ago keyed his nerve to the chance of interruption from some gun-brandishing householder; and to the possible pursuit of

226

police; and to the need of fighting or of fleeing. But all his preparations had not taken into account this newest emergency. He had not steeled himself to watch unmoved the gliding away of a treasure-satchel, apparently moving of its own will; nor the shimmer of two greenish sparks in the air just above it. And, for an instant, the man had to battle against a craven desire to bolt.

Lad, meanwhile, was having a beautiful time. Sincerely, he appreciated the playful grab his nocturnal friend had made in his direction. Lad had countered this, by frisking away for another five or six feet, and then wheeling about to face once more his playfellow and to await the next move in the blithe gambol. The pup could see tolerably well, in the darkness;—quite well enough to play the game his guest had devised. And of course, he had no way of knowing that the man could not see equally well.

Shaking off his momentary terror, the thief once more pressed the button of his flashlight; swinging the torch in a swift semi-circle and extinguishing it at once; lest the dim glow be seen by any wakeful member of the family.

That one quick sweep revealed to his gaze the shiny brown bag a half-dozen feet ahead of him, still swinging several inches above ground. He flung himself forward at it; refusing to believe he also saw that queer double glow of pale light, just above. He dived for the satchel with the speed and the accuracy of a football tackle. And that was all the good it did him.

227

Perhaps there is something in nature more agile and dismayingly elusive than a romping young collie. But that "something" is not a mortal man. As the thief sprang, Lad sprang in unison with him; darting to the left and a yard or so backward. He came to an expectant standstill once more; his tail wildly vibrating, his entire furry body tingling with the glad excitement of the game. This sportive visitor of his was a veritable godsend. If only he could be coaxed into coming to play with him every night—!

But presently he noted that the other seemed to have wearied of the game. After plunging through the air and landing on all fours with his grasping hands closing on nothingness, the man had remained thus, as if dazed, for a second or so. Then he had felt the ground all about him. Then, bewildered, he had scrambled to his feet. Now he was standing, moveless, his lips working.

Yes, he seemed to be tired of the lovely game—and just when Laddie was beginning to enter into the full spirit of it. Once in a while, the Mistress or the Master stopped playing, during the romps with the flannel doll. And Laddie had long since hit on a trick for reviving their interest. He employed this ruse now.

As the man stood, puzzled and scared, something brushed very lightly,—even coquettishly,—against his knuckles. He started in nervous fright. An instant later, the same thing brushed his knuckles again, this time more insistently. The man, in a spurt of fear-driven rage,

228

grabbed at the invisible object. His fingers slipped along the smooth sides of the bewitched bag that Lad was shoving invitingly at him.

Brief as was the contact, it was long enough for the thief's sensitive finger tips to recognise what they touched. And both hands were brought suddenly into play, in a mad snatch for the prize. The ten avid fingers missed the bag; and came together with clawing force. But, before they met, the finger tips of the left hand telegraphed to the man's brain that they had had momentary light experience with something hairy and warm —something that had slipped, eel-like, past them into the night;—something that most assuredly was no satchel, but *alive*!

The man's throat contracted, in gagging fright. And, as before, fear scourged him to feverish rage.

Recklessly he pressed the flashlight's button; and swung the muffled bar of light in every direction. In his other hand he levelled the pistol he had drawn. This time the shaded ray revealed to him not only his bag, but,— vaguely,—the Thing that held it.

He could not make out what manner of creature it was which gripped the satchel's handle and whose eyes pulsed back greenish flares into the torch's dim glow. But it was an animal of some kind;—distorted and formless in the wavering finger of blunted light, but still an animal. Not a ghost.

And fear departed. The intruder feared nothing mortal.

229

The mystery in part explained, he did not bother to puzzle out the remainder of it. Impossible as it seemed, his bag was carried by some living thing. All that remained for him was to capture the thing, and recover his bag. The weak light still turned on, he gave chase.

Lad's spirits arose with a bound. His ruse had succeeded. He had reawakened in this easily-discouraged chum a new interest in the game. And he gambolled across the lawn, fairly wriggling with delight. He did not wish to make his friend lose interest again. So instead of dashing off at full speed, he frisked daintily, just out of reach of the clawing hand.

And in this pleasant fashion the two playfellows covered a hundred yards of ground. More than once, the man came within an inch of his quarry. But always, by the most imperceptible spurt of speed, Laddie arranged to keep himself and his dear satchel from capture.

Then, in no time at all, the game ended; and with it ended Lad's baby faith in the friendliness and trustworthiness of all human nature.

Realising that the sound of his own stumbling running feet and the intermittent flashes of his torch might well awaken some light sleeper in the house, the thief resolved on a daring move. This creature in front of him,— dog or bear or goat, or whatever it was,—was uncatchable. But by sending a bullet through it, he could bring the animal to a sudden and permanent stop.

230

Then, snatching up his bag and running at top speed, he himself could easily win clear of the Place before any one of the household should appear. And his car would be a mile away before the neighbourhood could be aroused. Fury at the weird beast and the wrenching strain on his own nerves lent eagerness to his acceptance of the idea.

He reached back again for his pistol, whipped it out, and, coming to a standstill, aimed at the pup. Lad, waiting only to bound over an obstruction in his path, came to a corresponding pause, not ten feet ahead of his playmate.

It was an easy shot. Yet the bullet went several inches above the obligingly waiting dog's back. Nine men out of ten, shooting by moonlight or by flashlight, aim too high. The thief had heard this old marksman-maxim fifty times. But, like most hearers of maxims, he had forgotten it at the one time in his speckled career when it might have been of any use to him.

He had fired. He had missed. In another second, every sleeper in the house and in the gate-lodge would be out of bed. His night's work was a blank, unless—

With a bull rush he hurled himself forward at the interestedly waiting Lad. And, as he sprang, he fired again. Then several things happened.

Everyone, except movie actors and newly-appointed policemen, knows that a man on foot cannot shoot

231

straight, unless he is standing stock still. Yet, as luck would have it, this second shot found a mark where the first and better aimed bullet had gone wild.

Lad had leaped the narrow and deep ditch left along the lawn-edge by workers who were putting in a new water-main for the Place. On the far side of this obstacle he had stopped, and had waited for his friend to follow. But the friend had not followed. Instead, he had been somehow responsible for a spurt of red flame and for a most thrilling racket. Lad was more impressed than ever by the man's wondrous possibilities as a midnight entertainer. He waited, gaily expectant, for more. He got it.

There was a second rackety explosion and a second puff of lightning from the man's outflung hand. But, this time, something like a red-hot whip-lash smote Lad with horribly agonising force athwart the right hip.

The man had done this,—the man whom Laddie had thought so friendly and playful!

He had not done it by accident. For his hand had been outflung directly at the pup, just as once had been the arm of the kennelman, back at Lad's birthplace, in beating a disobedient mongrel. It was the only beating Lad had ever seen. And it had stuck, shudderingly, in his uncannily sensitive memory. Yet now, he himself had just had a like experience.

In an instant, the pup's trustful friendliness was gone. The man had come on the Place, at dead of night, and had struck him. That must be paid for! Never would the

232

pup forget his agonising lesson that night intruders are not to be trusted or even to be tolerated. Within a single second, he had graduated from a little friend of all the world, into a vigilant watchdog.

With a snarl, he dropped the bag and whizzed forward at his assailant. Needle-sharp milk teeth bared, head low, ruff abristle, friendly soft eyes as ferocious as a wolf's, he charged.

There had been scarce a breathing-space between the second report of the pistol and the collie's counter-attack. But there had been time enough for the onward-plunging thief to step into the narrow lip of the water-pipe ditch. The momentum of his own rush hurled the upper part of his body forward. But his left leg, caught between the ditch-sides, did not keep pace with the rest of him. There was a hideous snapping sound, a screech of mortal anguish; and the man crashed to earth, in a dead faint of pain and shock,—his broken left leg still thrust at an impossible angle in the ditch.

Lad checked himself midway in his own fierce charge. Teeth bare, throat agrowl, he hesitated. It had seemed to him right and natural to assail the man who had struck him so painfully. But now this same man was lying still and helpless under him. And the sporting instincts of a hundred generations of thoroughbreds cried out to him not to mangle the defenceless.

Wherefore, he stood, irresolute; alert for sign of movement on the part of his foe. But there was no such sign.

233

And the light bullet-graze on his hip was hurting like the very mischief.

Moreover, every window in the house beyond was blossoming forth into lights. There were sounds,—reassuring human sounds. And doors were opening. His deities were coming forth.

All at once, Laddie stopped being a vengeful beast of prey; and remembered that he was a very small and very much hurt and very lonely and worried puppy. He craved the Mistress's dear touch on his wound, and a word of crooning comfort from her soft voice. This yearning was mingled with a doubt lest perhaps he had been transgressing the Place's Law, in some new way; and lest he might have let himself in for a scolding. The Law was still so queer and so illogical!

Lad started toward the house. Then, pausing, he picked up the bag which had been so exhilarating a plaything for him this past few minutes and which he had forgotten in his pain.

It was Lad's collie way to pick up offerings (ranging from slippers to very dead fish) and to carry them to the Mistress. Sometimes he was petted for this. Sometimes the offering was lifted gingerly between aloof fingers and tossed back into the lake. But, nobody could well refuse so jingly and pretty a gift as this satchel.

The Master, sketchily attired, came running down the lawn, flashlight in hand. Past him, unnoticed, as he sped toward the ditch, a collie pup limped—a very unhappy and comfort-seeking puppy who carried in his mouth a blood-spattered brown bag.

"It doesn't make sense to me!" complained the Master, next day, as he told the story for the dozenth time, to a new group of callers. "I heard the shots and I went out to investigate. There he was lying half in and half out of the ditch. The fellow was unconscious. He didn't get his senses back till after the police came. Then he told some babbling yarn about a creature that had stolen his bag of loot and that had lured him to the ditch. He was all un-nerved and upset, and almost out of his head with pain. So the police had little enough trouble in 'sweating' him. He told everything he knew. And there's a whole-sale round-up of the motor-robbery bunch going on this afternoon as a result of it. But what I can't understand—"

"It's as clear as day," insisted the Mistress, stroking a silken head that pressed lovingly against her knee. "As clear as day. I was standing in the doorway here when Laddie came pattering up to me and laid a little satchel at my feet. I opened it, and—well, it had everything of value in it that had been in the safe over there. That and the thief's story make it perfectly plain. Laddie caught the man as he was climbing out of that window. He got the bag away from him; and the man chased him, firing as he went. And he stumbled into the ditch and—"

"Nonsense!" laughed the Master. "I'll grant all you say about Lad's being the most marvellous puppy on earth.

235

And I'll even believe all the miracles of his cleverness. But when it comes to taking a bag of jewelry from a burglar and then enticing him to a ditch and then coming back here to you with the bag—"

"Then how do you account—?"

"I don't. None of it makes sense to me. As I just said. But,—whatever happened, it's turned Laddie into a real watch dog. Did you notice how he went for the police when they started down the drive, last night? We've got a watchdog at last."

"We've got more than a watchdog," amended the Mistress. "An ordinary watchdog would just scare away thieves or bite them. Lad captured the thief and then brought the stolen jewelry back to us. No other dog could have done that."

Lad, enraptured by the note of praise in the Mistress's soft voice, looked adoringly up into the face that smiled so proudly down at him. Then, catching the sound of a step on the drive, he dashed out to bark in murderous fashion at a wholly harmless delivery boy whom he had seen every day for weeks.

A watchdog can't afford to relax vigilance, for a single instant,—especially at the responsible age of five months.

Wild Hunter

by K. C. RANDALL

Young Bob, coming back with the Warings in an early dusk, left them at the runs. Princess was in her kennel still. All afternoon he'd been afraid for what might happen to her. He handed the heavy game bag to Mr. Waring. It had been a good shoot. He had taken them to the right places and Duke had worked well and Mr. Waring had made some pretty kills. With Frank along to talk to and Mr. Waring happy over the guiding, it should have been almost as good as being out with Mr. Sewall and Mr. Doane and Princess.

But it wasn't. All afternoon in the back of Bob's mind was the fear that Princess might not be there when he came back to the runs. Frank wanted him to come to the main room and stay to supper with them. Mr. Waring urged this too, but Bob said no, that he had arranged with his Pop to pick him up about this time. What he really wanted to do was ask Mr. Doane if he had made up his mind about Princess. She was lying in the alley-

This story is from WILD HUNTER, by K. C. Randall

237

way of the kennel with her head down on her paws. When he spoke to her he could hear the slow thump of her tail, but she didn't come out.

Mr. Waring and Frank thanked him again and said they'd see him soon. They walked on to the main building, and Bob was just about to step over to the tack room when he heard the truck coming from the direction of the grounds. His Pop swung the door open, and Bob climbed up beside him. John Armitage seemed in a hurry and turned right around and gave the motor the gun.

They had to talk loud above the racket. Bob spoke of what was on his mind, asking his father if he'd heard about Princess.

"Yes," John Armitage said heavily. "I've heard. That was a shame what Ryder did to her. Al Doane has made up his mind to have her destroyed."

"He can't do that!" Bob cried. "He hasn't even tried to cure her!"

"Gun-shy at eight can't be cured, Al says."

"He's got to try, Pop." Bob's voice wasn't like any other his father had ever heard him use.

"Al Doane knows dogs," John Armitage said. "Furthermore, he's made up his mind. The vet is coming in the morning to take her away."

"I've got to see him!" Bob cried. "Turn around, Pop."

"What do you think you could do?" his father asked. He was driving more slowly now, and they could hear each other better.

 238

"I can try," Bob said. "I can ask Mr. Doane to let me try to break her."

It was so dark now that John Armitage switched on the lights. They were on a narrow sand road heavily crowded with brush and offering no place to turn.

"You mean bring her to the grounds?"

"Yes. Please turn around, Pop!"

"What about your mother? What will she say?"

It was just light enough in the cab of the old truck so that the father could see his son's face. The boy's cheeks were wet; he appeared to choke as though trying to speak, yet couldn't. John Armitage felt a tightening in his own throat. The road opened up at a pasture gate, and he swung the truck toward the bars and backed around.

"I'll take you back so you can talk to Al Doane," he said. "I'll drive right on home then and talk to your mother."

Bob took out his handkerchief and wiped his eyes. He didn't find his voice until they could see once more the lights of the Club. It was something of a marvel to John that the boy's tone, when he did speak, was so steady.

"Thank you, Pop," he said.

"I'll talk your mother into it," John Armitage said. "We'll be waiting up for you. Good luck with Al."

He rolled the truck up in front of the tack room.

Through the window they could see Al Doane in the rocker. Something white, the outline of a dog, crouched at his feet.

239

"He's got her up there with him!" John Armitage's voice showed his surprise.

Bob opened the cab door and let himself to the ground. His father watched the boy's short, stocky figure move steadily across the light to the door and reach up to knock.

"Good luck," he called to the boy again, and shifting gears with a grating roar, drove on toward the rearing grounds and a talk he didn't look forward to with Susan.

But Bob did not hear his father, just the low voice of Al Doane telling him to come in. He stood for a long moment half-blinded by the wall flare, and then his eyes let him see the old man in his splint rocker, Princess at his feet licking her wounds.

"I expected you, Bob," Al said. "What I have to tell you is a hard thing to say."

Bob said quickly: "I've heard, Mr. Doane. I heard from my Pop . . ."

"That the dog must go," Al said.

"I had Pop bring me back. There must be some other way for Princess. Something we can do for her."

"If there was a way, I'd try it," the old man said. "I haven't thought of any."

"There's me," Bob said. "I could try to break her. Give Princess to me!"

Al Doane smiled faintly. The boy's face, he could see, was pale and set, with smudges under the eyes that made him look older.

 240

"Ever handled a gun-shy dog, Bob?"

"No," Bob said, "but I could try."

"Trying isn't of much account. Not from my experience, anyway. She'd be no good to you or anyone else. Gun-shy at eight can't be cured. Been too good a dog to lose her self-respect and try to live without it."

Somewhere in the night a poacher's shot echoed and re-echoed. Princess shivered and whined, belly-crawled toward a dark corner.

"You see, Bob," Al said.

"I'd like to try to break her, Mr. Doane," the boy repeated. "I'll give up the hunting to work with her all the time."

He walked over, bent down close. Princess snarled deep in her throat as if she didn't know him, but young Bob did not flinch. His hand came lightly to the high dome and remained there while he spoke to her softly. In gloom outside the flare, white showed from rolling eyes; but the dog remained quiet.

Al Doane said: "Bring her back into the light."

Young Bob stood up.

"Heel, Princess." He turned and came toward Al, who sat watching him closely, troubled over that round face so unnaturally white in the harsh brilliance let down by the flare.

A slow scratching told that Princess had stood and was following stiffly.

And seeing them there together, Al thought once again

241

of Ryder and his money that seemed to buy anything, and of the difference between these two and the sport. And there came to him the question: What harm would it do if he did humor the boy? It might not matter if a little time were given. He had Princess here tonight out of dread of tomorrow, not wanting to let her go. A little more time—for her and the boy. Would it matter in the long run to do the kindly thing? His voice told nothing when he said: "Hasn't forgotten her manners. At least she minds you, Bob."

"You'll let me have Princess?" Bob asked. His voice was trembling now. "Please, Mr Doane."

The old man said slowly, as though reluctant still: "I will on certain conditions, although by all I know about dogs, I shouldn't."

Bob's face glowed like a light breaking out of the dark, and now his voice was steady.

"I'd like her outright to make her absolutely safe."

Al Doane shook his head.

"This afternoon I took a thousand dollars from the one who shot her. He paid with the understanding she never could hunt again, and I gave word to do what in my judgment was the right thing."

He lit a second flare on the high far wall. It picked up brass of sulky harness, brought alive the pacing beauty of Dan Patch—a colored lithograph under glass. The gun rack just below became a soft shine of brown barrels and hand-rubbed walnut. Al took down a light sixteen-gauge Parker double, its metal gleaming dull like wet silk.

"Time you had a bigger gun, Bob," he said. "Seems like by another season you'll have outgrown your .410. Let's see how this one fits you."

He stood holding the gun, looking steadily at Bob. "See here," he said, "I can't give Princess outright, but we'll strike up a fair bargain. This date next year you run her in the first field, opening morning. If she's steady to shot, you can step in here and take down this gun for your own."

Bob's face didn't light up again the way a twelve year-old's should. He did not move to take the sixteen from Al's hands.

"It's a beauty of a gun," he said slowly. "Like the very one I've always wanted, but I'd rather have Princess to keep." His voice came up high with a break in it. "You've told me you will have her destroyed."

"Yes," Al said. "That's what I had planned to do. Ryder understood that when I took his check. There was no choice for him but to pay, having done what he did. Jim Sewall and the Club Committee helped set the figure. It was their understanding too. I shall have her destroyed if you fail to break her."

"I don't care if she never hunts again," Bob said.

"Look at her," the old man said.

243

The setter had given up licking herself and sat at their feet mournfully, her head down as though she were ready to cringe and crawl back into her corner.

"I don't care," Bob said again. "She won't always be like this, even if she's still gun-shy."

Al Doane laid the Parker back in the rack.

"I care," he said. "That's what she was whelped for. Pride in herself and in the hunting. That and no more."

The boy said: "Don't you think there's any chance for her and me?"

"No," Al said. "I don't. But you've wheedled me into letting you try. Your father's place over at the rearing grounds is quiet—away from most of the shooting—." He broke off speaking, looked at his watch. "It's late. I'll have Joe Means run you and Princess home in the pick-up."

Princess went with young Bob willingly enough, and when the harsh roar of the truck had died, Al Doane stepped back into the tack room and drew the rocker to its accustomed place by the window. From this point of vantage he could see the kennels, their whitewashed houses lit by a frosty October moon. The king's run would be empty again, and from all he knew about dogs and the training of them, there'd come a time when the name PRINCESS would come down from it for good.

Maybe he'd been too hasty. A greater heartbreak for the boy might be all that would come from this reprieve for the setter. A little more time for them both. Was it worth the try? He hoped so, but couldn't feel right about

244

it all. Time would tell, as it always did. He looked again at his watch in its fat silver case. Not much after nine; it seemed much later. The members were still up, and he'd be willing to place a wager as to what they were talking about. Somehow he didn't feel like stepping across to tell of this new development. And yet it was a relief to put off what tomorrow had been due to bring.

And now young Bob, having won reprieve for Princess, began the discouraging task of breaking her. Jim Sewall made it a point to keep in touch with the boy's progress. John Armitage, closer now than he had ever been to his son, was at the Club building nearly every day, and Jim never failed to ask about Bob and Princess. Al Doane, once having changed his mind, appeared to put the whole matter from him as though content to wait, as he saw it, for the boy's inevitable failure. An arrangement was made whereby Bob came to the Club only to carry for Jim Sewall; the time formerly spent about the kennels was given over to Princess. The two old men no longer hunted together. With Princess gone from the king's suite Al Doane seemed to lose interest in the hunting. He now spent his time working with Duke, the big blue belton, readying him for the challenge match set by Ryder. And he did not appear to want Jim's company in this work with Duke.

That night of opening day, John Armitage, driving home ahead of Bob, was able to prepare an unwilling

245

Susan for the possible arrival of Princess. They were still at table when tires crunched on gravel and voices sounded outside, along with a low barking.

"He was able to bring her," John Armitage said. "You'll let the boy have his way, Susan, as to where he'll keep Princess."

He sat facing the door, his shoulders heavy in a checked wool shirt, his iron-grey hair silvery in the lamplight. Susan Armitage bustled to set a place for Bob. As usual she was scrubbed-looking and pink-faced and neat in starched gingham and white apron.

"He'll want her in his room," she said.

"Let him, then, until we can set up a kennel and run. Bob might as well start in right to win her confidence. I've heard plenty of stories at the Club how bull-headed she is. Only Al Doane himself can hunt her, and in the training he near had to kill her before she'd obey him."

"Land sakes!" Susan Armitage exclaimed. "Why does Bob want a dog like that around?"

"It will be good for him to try to handle her all by himself," John said. "And that, as I've told you, seems what he most wants to do. Last year he carried for Jim Sewall and Al and of course watched Princess in the field. It's tickled me no end the way he's stood up to Al Doane over her."

They could hear the truck driving away and Bob's steps on the boards of the back porch along with a slow scratching.

"Princess won't be very lively tonight," John Armitage told Susan. "She was hurt bad in the morning."

Bob stood in the doorway, and Susan could see the dog at his side, head down and using her forelegs stiffly to cross the sill. Bob's eyes were shining, proud and happy.

"I've got her, Pop," he cried. "That is, until I can break her."

"Al didn't give outright?" John Armitage was disappointed. "But I wouldn't blame him. She's a famous dog in these parts already."

"I've saved her, anyway," Bob said. "Down, Princess."

The setter limped to the stove and let herself down with a dead thud on the scrubbed boards. She looked up at Bob, and her tail beat feebly.

"My, how poor she is!" Susan exclaimed. "I'll have to get her a pan of warm milk."

John Armitage winked at Bob, but was careful not to let his wife see him.

"Sit down. Supper's on the stove. Your mother will take charge of the dog."

Susan Armitage bustled at the range, warming the milk.

John Armitage winked at Bob again: "Looks like Princess will be getting fed first. I can see you're going to have a coddled, spoiled dog on your hands, son."

And so started the new relationship for Bob and Princess.

247

Princess was to sleep that night on a rug laid by the stove. It was long past Bob's bedtime, but he made excuses to stay with her, dawdling over his supper, eating and eating, until Susan, who watched his appetite closely, had to protest.

"Maybe I should sleep here on a cot," Bob suggested. "Princess will feel so strange, and I'm the only one she really knows."

"Nonsense," Susan Armitage said. "She's half asleep already."

The setter had her head down on her paws, appearing to doze. Every so often she cried and whimpered in this half-sleep.

John Armitage yawned and stretched.

"Better get to bed, son. You'll want to be up bright and early to tend her."

Bob left the table reluctantly, but when he did so and said good night and opened the door leading to his room, Princess scrambled up painfully and followed.

"No, Princess! No!" Bob said.

He came back and knelt by the rug and tried to make her lie down. But she had sensed his leaving, and while she crouched on the rug, her stay before the stove was uneasy. When Bob stood again, she stood and followed.

"That's just how I thought it would be," Susan Armitage complained. "She'll keep us up all night."

"Now, Mother." John Armitage was smiling. "There's

 248

no need for you to stay awake. I think perhaps she'll try to follow Bob upstairs."

Bob went again to the door and mounted the steep lifts slowly. Princess stood for a moment looking up, and then followed, taking the treads with a torturing heave of her forelegs.

Susan Armitage came after, giving directions.

"Get that old horse blanket in the back shed, John, and then we'll want a drawer from the pine bureau in the attic."

From somewhere she whisked out a discarded feather pillow and laid it in the drawer and spread the blanket.

"You get undressed now, Robert, and climb into bed, or she'll never quiet down."

"How about you, Mother?" John Armitage asked. "I haven't seen you so excited since Cousin Clara's last visit."

Susan sniffed audibly.

"Come along, John. We'll leave them up here and hope for the best."

Princess had been exploring the room, but she came now at Bob's command and lay down in her nest. He climbed onto the high bed, peering from its footboard to let her know where he was. She seemed to sense that he would stay near her. After one try to scramble up to him, she returned to the blanket and settled for the night.

249

It was a long time before Bob could get to sleep. Moonlight came in the windows, flooding pale light on the counterpane. The setter was asleep. He could hear the faint sound of her breathing, with now and then a weak whimper as though bad dreams frightened her. The covers felt warm and heavy. Carefully he pushed back the outer one and crawled again to the footboard to look down to make sure she was all right. Before he dropped off to sleep he made many plans for them both. But first Princess would have to get strong and well again.

In the morning she was so stiff and sore that they had to carry her downstairs. John Armitage said it was a blessing she wasn't a Great Dane or a Saint Bernard.

Susan surprised her men by suggesting that Bob stay home from church to tend the setter. It was a fine sunny day, and he brought the rug out on the flagstones by the kitchen door. Susan had prepared warm milk and table scraps, but Princess wouldn't eat. She lay all day in the sun, dozing and whining in her sleep, and Bob stayed close by. Toward evening she seemed easier and walked slowly with him about the yard. When he brought her in toward dusk, she cleaned up her dish and rested again until time to go upstairs.

Monday was a school day, and Bob, called early by his father, helped Princess down the stairs, and she followed him to the barn. At first she was in the way when he tried to clean the stalls, but soon learned to watch from a little distance. When he fed the hens, she was at his heels, but made no move to follow into the chicken yard.

His father stood in the barn door to watch.

"She's well behaved," he said. "You can tell she's lived on a farm."

"Princess won't have to drive any more cows," Bob said stoutly. "She's a hunting dog, Pop."

"That's right," John Armitage said. "I wasn't figuring to put her back where she started. Seems better this morning, don't she?"

"Yes," Bob said. "She's a lot better. In another day or two I can run her after school."

He bent down, pride in his eyes, and patted the setter's head.

"What about school?" John asked. "What will she do with you away all day?"

"I hadn't thought of that!" Bob exclaimed. "How can I leave her so soon, Pop?"

"Maybe your mother will have some plan or other," John suggested. "We'll ask her at breakfast. We may have to tie Princess this first morning."

"Couldn't I take her to school?" Bob asked. "She'd be awfully quiet."

In the end they had to tie Princess those first few mornings. She strained and barked, and it was hard for Bob to leave her. But in an hour she quieted, and when Susan untied and fed her, made no move to run away.

All day the setter dozed on her rug on the warm stones. When the school bus stopped at the mailbox that first

251

afternoon at a quarter to four, she raised her head and saw Bob running up the drive. Stiffly she limped to meet him, trying to wriggle like a pup and barking her welcome. Each day after that, when a quarter to four came, she grew uneasy, lifting up to watch for the bus; and when it showed on the road, she left her stand and loped down drive to meet it. Each day found her feeding better and the stiffness leaving her forelegs. All during the time until dark when Bob helped his father with the chores, she followed close at his heels. That week he didn't accomplish much. He spent most of his time petting Princess and talking to her about the many things he'd planned when they could go into the fields.

At this time of year John Armitage cut corn and filled his silo. He had hired a blower rig to draw in on Friday and finish Saturday morning. The blower was powered by an ancient engine long past its prime. A fan belt had to be replaced, and it was near noon before the crew had set up the filling. Princess out on her rug had paid little attention to the commotion at the barn, and John Armitage and Susan, busier than ever, forgot the setter. The rust-crusted engine had to be cranked, starting up ponderously with a series of backfirings like rifle shots. No one in the yard or the house saw Princess cower down whimpering, and then run around the corner of the house and on past the barnyard.

When Bob, eager with Friday plans for a trip into the

fields, clambered from the bus, Princess did not come down the drive to meet him. He ran now, bursting into the kitchen where Susan peeled potatoes for supper.

"Where's Princess, Mom?" he cried. "She's gone!"

Susan stood and looked through the window.

"I couldn't say. I've been so busy with feeding the silo men and cleaning up I just haven't kept track of her. She's never run off before. Maybe she's out by the barn with the men."

Out in the yard the heavy roar of the blower diminished and stopped. Almost at once they heard the heavy backfiring as the cranked engine fired and caught.

"That's it!" Bob cried. "Princess heard the backfire and ran away!"

He was out of the house, running toward the crew below the silo. John Armitage had just driven up with a high-piled load of shocks and had to lean far over in the racket of the blower to hear Bob's voice.

"I haven't seen Princess," John said. "I quite forgot about her, son. She's probably not run far. Crawled under something, maybe, and of course she won't come out."

"I've got to find her, Pop!"

"I'd counted on you to tread ensilage up in the silo, but you go ahead. Look in the barn cellar, or out in the carriage house."

Bob didn't stop to change his clothes. It was a dusty

253

business, poking here and there where a dog might hide, but the most likely places were empty. He called "Princess" until his throat felt raw and all choked up. An hour and a half went by, and the crew shut off the engine and got into their cars to go home. John Armitage had chores to do, but put them off to help look. Susan, a shawl over her head, came out to make suggestions.

"When they run away like Princess has, do they go a long way?" Bob asked. His voice was choked and trembling.

"I don't think so," John Armitage told him. "I'd say she'd crawl into the first place she came to."

"But I've looked everywhere," Bob said.

"There's the old wheat stack back of the barn," Susan suggested. "Did you look there?"

Bob was gone almost before she had the words out of her mouth.

The stack, he now remembered, had caves in it where the hogs had rooted. He'd hid in one once himself. The first was empty. He called again, his voice hoarse and unnatural. On the far side was another opening, fringed with straw and dark inside. Bending down he thought he saw the shine of eyes, and then a low-growling mutter struck his ears. The opening wasn't too large, but it hollowed out farther in. A briar scratched his face, and a dusty bite of chaff dust made him sneeze. Princess was there, all right. His eyes accustomed to the dark, he could see the pale blur of her white coat.

He spoke to her softly.

"Come, girl. Steady, girl. I've come to find you."

The setter shifted. She wasn't really growling now, just whining. And when he came close, so that his head was down by hers, the warm, rough sandpaper of her tongue was on his cheek.

He didn't try to bring her out at first. It was enough to have found her, to know she hadn't really run away. And now Susan's voice was calling him, and keeping his hand on Princess' collar, he tugged gently and drew her out into the open. She had her head up now, listening, but the early evening air was still.

Bob didn't tread ensilage on Saturday. Long before the crew came back he took Princess to a far corner of the grounds. There was a little stream that ran brown and sparkling through a wood, and the day was warm enough so that he took off his shoes and socks and hung them around his neck and waded along the low bank looking for shiners, the dog following in the grass.

"Come on in, Princess," he called.

They had come to a natural dam of down logs which had widened the stream into a shallow pool. A brown trout arrowed ahead and hid in deeper water. Bob rolled his overalls as high as they would go and crossed to the other side as though to climb the bank. Princess began to stamp and bark.

"Come on, Princess. We're going into the next field."

He was nearly across when he heard the splash of her

255

jump. In the middle the water was just deep enough to make her swim with her head showing sleek and wet like a beaver's. Bob pulled himself up by an overhanging branch, but the setter had to swim farther up to cross. She came crashing through the brush, soaked and dripping, and when he sat down in the sun to put on his shoes, she shook herself to give him a regular shower, and then rolled and squirmed at his feet to dry her coat.

It was so nice here with the warm sun dappling down through the fall leaves of water elms and tall maples all yellow and fire-red that he didn't want to go home.

"If we'd thought to bring a lunch, we could stay all day, Princess," he told her.

The setter gave up rolling and came over to lick his face.

"We could pretend we were on an island like Robinson Crusoe was—away from everybody, and you could be my man Friday; and we'd have to build a hut out of branches and rub sticks together to make a fire, and then maybe we'd go hunting for a rabbit or a bird for supper."

Princess sat up at the word bird. She had her head cocked to one side with one ear rolled over like a little cap.

"Wouldn't we, Princess?"

The setter gave a light bark.

"Or maybe we'd have to go fishing for that trout in the pool the way they do on real desert islands, but you'd rather hunt for birds, wouldn't you?"

 256

Princess barked again and ran a little way into the woods, turned to stamp her feet as though she wanted something.

"Would you like to go hunting? Do you think we could find a bird in the next field? We'll see what's in back of the woods."

They came out into a great rolling acreage of wheat stubble cut high by the combine. For the first time since her stay at the grounds the setter circled away to hunt. She seemed to forget all about Bob, who stood watching her run just as on that day when Mr. Doane and he had seen her on the clover. Bob at the edge of the wheat watched Princess grow smaller and smaller. She was starting to circle back now. He wondered if he shouldn't call her in, just to see if she'd obey. And then he saw birds in the air, a flock of six or eight with the roosters burnished golden by the sun, the setter following until she was out of sight. Bob ran toward where the ground rolled higher. Now he could see her, still running hard, wild hunting. Another flock rose; farther on, a single.

He called now, but was afraid she couldn't hear. If only he'd brought the .410. Maybe in the wild hunting she'd forget about the gun sound. It was a big field, and she must have covered all of it before he saw her again, coming in more slowly, panting hard when she reached him.

He stooped to rub her ears and work out a patch of burs on her neck.

257

"That was fun, wasn't it, girl?" he said. "Next time we'll bring the gun along."

The sun was straight overhead, and he knew it was time to start for home. Princess stayed at heel most of the way back. When he was near enough to the buildings, he listened hard for the blower, but the crew had gone.

All next week after school he had her out in the cover. As Al Doane had said, it was quiet at the grounds away from the shooting, but there were a few birds closer in than the wheat-field beyond the woods. Princess continued the wild hunting; but one day she caught a weak flyer and brought it to Bob. He held her by the neck and praised and petted her. And when he let her go, she circled again, but this time waited on the field, holding the pheasant under her nose, an eye rolling toward Bob coming up.

All week he'd been carrying the .410 without quite daring to fire it; but this time when the bird rose, he fired and dropped it, his heart in his throat for what Princess would do.

And with the light roar, the savage stiffness of her stand melted. She whined as though the shot had torn into her, and then, as on that opening morning, ran from the field. Bob called and called, but she did not stop. With his father he had been working on her kennel and run, and a half-hour later found her in the straw, still shaking as though from cold. It was an hour before he could coax her to him and into the house.

All through supper Princess was uneasy, leaving her place by the stove, whining and crying in her throat.

"Mercy on us, what ails that dog?" Susan Armitage asked.

Bob, picking at a plate of pheasant and dressing, said nothing.

"You tried to shoot over her," John Armitage pointed out.

"She ran away," Bob blurted. "Just like she did opening day."

"They don't forget gun-shyness," his father said. "Especially if they've been hurt bad like this one. I'm surprised she'll even go into the fields, let alone point a bird. But then, Princess is no ordinary dog. I've spoken to Jim Sewall and Al Doane. They say you'll have to starve her."

"I can't do that, Pop."

"My, no!" Susan Armitage looked shocked. "I'm just beginning to get a little flesh on her."

"It's the only way. Sometimes it works."

"I can't do it, Pop," Bob said again.

"You took her to break her. If you don't, Al Doane will have her back and . . ."

"I know." Bob's voice was unsteady. "I can't eat any more, Mom. I'll take Princess upstairs."

"You think about what I've told you," John Armitage said.

In Bob's room Princess went to her blanket, and he

259

sat on the rug beside her. She lifted her head and ran a rough tongue across his cheek.

"I can't do it, Princess," he said. "I just can't."

Those dark and knowing eyes looked up at him trustfully. He could hear the soft beat of her tail against the wooden end of the drawer. She licked his face again, and then he couldn't talk any more or see her very well either.

But later that night, lying awake with the October moonlight white across his bedspread, he knew there was no other way. Mr. Doane had told his father about the starving and he was head guide and handler at the Club, a man old and wise. A thought came to the boy that Al Doane with his knowledge of dogs and hunting hadn't been willing even to try to save Princess, believing that she was too old to be broken. He could hear her below him on her blanket, snoring and wheezing just a little in her sleep. He'd been going to church every Sunday since he could remember. His mother, when he was younger, used to come up to hear his prayers. She didn't anymore, although she sometimes asked if he was remembering to pray each night. Sometimes he forgot, as he had tonight. But maybe, just maybe, it would help if he asked God to cure Princess. He slipped out of bed and knelt on the cold floor the way he used to with his mother. He felt a little better after he had made his prayer. He could see Princess, curled up and still

260

asleep. He wanted to smooth her head, but was afraid he'd wake her.

When he did go to sleep, he had a nightmare. Al Doane was in it and Mr. Sewall and Princess. They were looking at him, sternly saying the time was growing short and that Princess would have to be starved. He stood before them not knowing what to say. And then Mr. Doane took from his pocket a dog leash. Princess was suddenly looking up at him, and Mr. Doane took a step toward them both and snapped the leash on her collar; and the two old men led her away. They seemed to be moving into a blazing light from the sun. Once Princess looked back and made as if to pull away from them and run back to him. But Mr. Doane held the leash, and then they were gone.

He woke up calling "Princess." It was daylight in the room with the sun on his face, and her head and paws showed on the covers as she tried to climb up on the high, old-fashioned bed. The dream had been so real that he could hardly believe she was here beside him. He slid down beside her and put his arm around her neck.

"I'll have to do it, Princess," he said. "I don't want to. You mustn't ever think I want to, but there's no other way."

The dream seemed real even while he was dressing. He was glad it was Sunday, and he wouldn't be going to the Club where he would see Mr. Doane and Mr. Sewall.

261

At breakfast he told his Pop that he would try the starving. John Armitage said he had a book on training and breaking that he'd brought from the Club. They read it together, the directions that said so flatly what to do in the case of a gun-shy dog. According to the author, a well-known handler, it would take five days, and if at the end of that time the starving had failed, the chances of breaking would be pretty hopeless. Princess was to be offered food once every twenty-four hours. She would be kept in her run. At each feeding time a shot would be fired, at first from quite a distance. If she left her food, it would be taken away for twenty-four hours until the try could be made again.

It was a bad five days. The worst Bob could remember. And the starving didn't work. Princess couldn't be broken by taking away her food. She would lie in the kennel, and when Bob set down the dish, rush to it, and back away at the sound of the shot, although John Armitage stood a long way off with the .410. They went beyond the five days into a full week. Princess, already honed down by her training, faded fast to a skeleton of barrel-like ribs, thin as a case knife across the loins.

It was Susan Armitage who put a stop to it, appearing before them in the yard, her eyes afire with determination. She marched straight to Bob and took the dish from his hands.

"Put away that gun, John Armitage," she called loudly. "I won't have any more of this cruelty to Princess.

The both of you have carried your foolishness far enough."

John Armitage stood by sheepishly while Susan fed the setter and led her into the house. But Bob, knowing now that the starving had failed, followed closely, his eyes so wet he could hardly see where he was going.

That evening Bob had a talk with his father and mother. He was feeling so discouraged that when Mom brought on the Sunday night snack of milk and pumpkin pie, he said he didn't want any. Princess was asleep in front of the stove. She was so thin and her coat so rough and lifeless-looking that he could hardly bear to look at her. Mom was cheerful and spoke of building her up again, but Pop, who hadn't forgotten the deal with Al Doane, was as gloomy as Bob.

"It didn't work," Pop said. "Al Doane, with all his experience, was right. He had no real faith in the starving. She was hurt too bad. It'll take a miracle to break her. We know now that starving won't do it."

"What kind of miracle," Bob asked. "Like those you read about in the Bible?"

"I don't know any more than you. I'm about ready to believe the days of miracles are over."

"That's sacrilegious, John." Susan Armitage was severe. "You heard what the pastor said this morning. Or were you asleep?"

"I heard him," Pop mumbled, "and Bob did too. But that isn't going to help this dog any."

263

"It will work out all right." Susan Armitage spoke confidently. "Al Doane will end up by giving Princess to Bob. If he doesn't, he's going to hear a piece of my mind."

"That won't do any good," John Armitage said. "Al Doane is bound by his agreement, and he's a man of his word. I can say only this. Bob should take the setter back to Al and have it over with, first as last. It won't be an easy thing to do, but later it will be much harder. More so, maybe, than he can stand."

"I'll go see Mr. Doane myself," Bob's voice was confident, too.

"I wouldn't," his father said. "I've just said Al Doane is bound by his word. He'll not go back on that, once he's given it. You won't get anywhere with him this time."

"I could try."

John Armitage spoke more strongly. "I wouldn't. You've had your chance. You won't be well thought of by Al, or Mr. Sewall either, if you don't stand by your agreement."

"Your father's right," Susan Armitage said. "I can see that now, Robert. You'll only make things harder for Mr. Doane if he has to refuse you."

Bob's round face had set in lines that reminded John Armitage of Susan when some member of the Ladies' Aid crossed her.

"I'd like to wait a little longer, Pop. I won't give Princess up quite yet."

264

"You're making it harder for yourself each day you wait," his father told him. "I'll not advise you further about her."

A little later Bob took Princess out to the kennel. Susan had prepared a second dish of warm milk and table scraps. When he set it down Princess eyed him warily, as if half expecting to hear a shot that would drive her from it. She crept closer and at last was wolfing her supper. Bob watched over her, holding a flashlight until the dish was clean. He was kneeling down, and she came and rubbed her wet muzzle across his cheek, her dark eyes pleading for more.

"No, Princess," he said. "No more for now. You haven't eaten for so long we don't dare feed you what you'd like to have."

She crouched down, and her tail beat feebly in the dust of the yard.

"Maybe a miracle will happen to you and me, Princess. It's our only chance. Maybe if we wait a little longer it will happen."

Princess seemed to agree, for the tail-thumping grew stronger. Bob brought her back into the house and said good night to Mom and Pop, and Princess followed him upstairs. It was hard for her to climb now, she was so weak. She settled on her blanket, and Bob undressed and then gave her a last pat before climbing into bed. He said once more: "Maybe if we wait a little longer, Princess, it will happen."

265

But he really didn't believe what he had said to her. He remembered the night before they began the starving when she had come upstairs with him, and he had prayed for her to be cured. And all that happened was a bad nightmare that had frightened him and made him glad to wake up into sunshine and Princess still in the room. He remembered Al Doane's face—more than ever like the face of the Indian Chieftain—and how the eyes, so sharp and hard, had looked at Princess and at him before the two old men had led her away. Pop had spoken of a miracle, but wasn't at all hopeful that they ever happened any more. Nor was he, either.

He went back to running Princess in the fields after school, carrying the .410 but never firing it. A hunter, strange to the grounds, had he met them while out for an evening shoot, would not have been impressed. He would have seen only a stocky, round-faced boy in overalls and faded canvas coat, running an under-sized setter, terribly thin and out of condition.

Jim Sewall still asked about Princess whenever Bob carried for him, and the news was never good. Al Doane, with troubles of his own as the field trial drew nearer, seemed to have put Princess completely from his mind. He never asked Bob how she was doing. He had, of course, learned from John Armitage that the starving had failed to break her. Upon hearing this the old man had merely shaken his head and turned their talk to other matters.

266

For an instant she seemed to writhe under those great
stomping hoofs

267

John Armitage, among his other duties connected with the Club, kept the work horses pastured on his place. On an overcast afternoon, Bob and Princess, crossing into the south pasture, came on a big roan gelding feeding close to the fence corner. He was a Percheron and Belgian cross, and old, with white showing on the heavy Roman nose. He had been let out to pasture because of a collar gall that had infected and swelled into a great bunch high on the withers.

Princess, feeding well now, had begun to fill out and grow glossy in the coat. She circled away strongly, cutting toward the horse, and he went for her, catching her by surprise, so that for an instant the white coat seemed to writhe under those great stomping hoofs. Bob ran at the horse shouting, and it wheeled ponderously and came for him at a lunging gallop.

He turned and ran for the fence, shivers of fear cold up and down his back, hearing that heavy pounding, muffled and thunderous on the frosty sod, closing upon him.

And then Princess barked. He looked back to see a savage leap at those trampling forelegs that smashed close in to where her white coat flashed. One of them must have grazed her, for she rolled away with a shrill whimper. Bob stood now and snap-shot at the roan, the .410 held at his waist and pointed without aiming at the reddish bulk of the horse. The pattern edge, just a fine shot or two, must have struck and stung the big gelding; for he wheeled again and bucked down field. Princess was up

268

watching, stiffened out almost as if on point. With trembling finger Bob squeezed the second trigger, firing again over a dog that gave no heed to the sound. Now he called to her, and she came with him through the fence.

He felt weak in the knees and had to sit on a stump, Princess at his feet, panting as if from a hard run. It came over him that the miracle had happened. She wouldn't be shy any more of gun sound. It had taken more than the starving. What he felt for her was in it; and she had wanted to protect him. When he was in that great danger from the roan, running for his life, she had sensed it all and cut in again under those pounding hoofs to slow them. That he had thought to fire the .410 a second time was a part of the miracle too.

He said over and over again like a boy who has awakened from the shock of a dream: "You're cured, Princess. You're cured!"

The gun across his knees had slipped down a little, and he broke it open and reached for shells to reload. The feel of cold metal steadied him, made him think of Pop and Mom and the need to hurry home to tell them. And then, for no reason, he heard, as though he were back at the Club, the calm voice of Al Doane saying: "We'll see." And as suddenly he wasn't sure. Princess, so quiet a moment before, stirred uneasily, thrust her forepaw against his leg. He'd have to try her again. Better to be sure. It meant so much to them both. He sat for a long time petting her, holding hard to the .410 with one hand.

269

Then he stood and brought her to heel, walking a few paces before letting her circle out. Princess wasn't far from the gun when he brought it up and in his fumbling fear touched off both barrels. But she did not flinch. Her head turned just a little as though in wonderment at what he was doing.

He was down on his knees now, calling her, his arms around her, and he could feel her rough tongue on his cheek. It had happened—the miracle really had happened! He was sure of it now.

M. deV. Lee

#10365